Compilation

A Collection of Short Stories

David Peters

Divergent Mind Books

First paperback edition 2025

ISBN: 978-1-7394124-7-0

Contents

The Strix

The sunlight on his face startled him awake, disrupting his dreams of faraway places and long-ago times. Before opening his eyes, the aroma of freshly made coffee caused his mind to drift back to the happy times he had spent in Dozza (a small town not too far from Bologna, Italy). Every night had been joyous amongst the company of friendly villagers at the Osteria, where he had fallen in love with Francesca. He spent every day working on the new aqueduct and, every night, escaped the world into her understanding eyes. An age had passed since, but his love for Francesca had not. Reality spurned away the last ebbs of his dream as the radio alarm sprang to life, 'Good morning, San Francisco. It's twenty-two degrees outside, and there are huge tailbacks on the Central Freeway due to an accident, so a late start at work for many commuters today!' Mikhael realised that simple life was in the past; today was just an ever-moving flow of actions in a world of analysts. Forcing a smile onto his face, he told himself, 'Today is a beautiful day!' He enjoyed the sun's warmth on his face, the drifting scent of freshly picked Gardenia and the aroma of coffee. 'It does my soul good!' he spoke aloud, re-instilling in himself the valued counsel of an old friend. For life had not always been pleasant. Indeed, there had been many times when simply clinging to something small, like the fragrant smell of Gardenia, had kept him sane. His family were Strix, as they had been known in the old times, back in ancient Greece, or Vampires, as the modern world knows them today. Cultures had changed in so many ways since those early days in

Greece when the slightest suspicion of vampiric nature saw them murdered or driven out of town. In those days, he had stayed in the shadows, only appearing at night when the dim lamp lights disguised his pale complexion. Society today does neither fear nor care about Vampires. Just as the suppression of women had been forgotten by today's generation, so too had his kind been forgotten, existing only in fairy stories, an absurd footnote of history. Yet despite this new freedom, Mikhael despised the modern culture for all its differences from the old. He felt lost and abandoned by the old Gods and yearned to return to ancient Athens.

He had to be at work by nine, so he made the most of his time with his wife and daughter before rushing off. Savouring every giggle and even every scorn from Belinda, who at times could worry the most fearless vampire with her retained teenage frustrations. As a Professor of Archaeology and working at the prestigious Museum Legion of Honor, he found himself wandering in the Hall of Antiquities every day, reminiscing about his early life. He liked to remind himself that he was human, of his early aspirations and endurances. Sometimes, he found himself educating visitors about the relics he so strongly felt connected to.

Life now was so different from his life growing up, yet, in some ways, the same. The law courts operated in a similar fashion. Juries were, of course, smaller, and they still claimed to carry out absolute justice just as they had in ancient Greece. Everyone still complained about unjust laws, never stopping for a moment to consider the interference of an unjust judge or jury! The more things change, the more they stay the same, he thought to himself.

Today, he was to meet Dr. Frederick Hausen from the Metropolitan Museum of Art, a gentleman who touted a great knowledge of ancient Greek culture. Hoping against hope that this gentleman would be as knowledgeable as he had so often claimed in the academic press, Mikhael waited by a Black-Glazed Greek Lamp for the Doctor. Standing silently, looking at the lamp, he could remember the smell of the oil burning in the air on that final night he had seen his wise mentor and friend. He secretly yearned to tell the world about his former mentor Socrates and how, through many late-night parties, Socrates had guided Mikhael to question his fears and place within this world. Of all the mortals he had met, Socrates had been only one of two people he had ever confided in about his curse. He was guided to see he was no less human than any other man, that his actions rather than his life force made him who he was. He recalled the questioning of his mentor in directing his thoughts when he explained about his demons, 'Are you a good man now?' enquired Socrates. 'I try to be, but sometimes the urge to feed is so strong I must do it!' 'And what do you kill? What do you feed on Mikhael?' 'I feed on cattle.' 'Do you agree, Mikael, that we all must eat, that this is but a basic human requirement?' 'Yes.' 'When you develop this urge, is it to feed on cattle?' 'No, it is for human blood!' 'I think, Mikhael, that if one puts forward your theory, then we are forced to deny that any man who has a bad thought whatsoever could be a good man despite his actions.' 'It's not the same.' Argued Mikhael. 'Perhaps I'm to blame. Maybe I did not explain myself clearly. If a man is enraged with another to the point of desiring his death, yet does not act upon this desire and does not kill his fellow man, is he acting in good character or bad character?' 'Good character.' Admitted Mikhael. 'And I agree. Do you have the strength needed to kill another man; would this be a difficult physical feat for you?' 'No, it would be easy.' 'Then let me ask you this in that case. Is a man who doesn't do something which is easy, because it is wrong, a good or bad person?' 'A good person, b...' Mikhael was interrupted as Socrates continued his line of thought. 'I agree with you, Mikhael. It is the trait of good character. So, do you agree with me that we all must feed and nourish ourselves, that this is a human state, and without such, we would each die?' 'Yes, b...' 'Hold on, then. We

5

agree that we all must nourish ourselves and that avoiding killing our fellow man, regardless of desire or urge, is a trait of good character. Now, I have only ever met one Strix, you, Mikhael, but my understanding is that Striges kill their fellow man without consideration. Is that true?' 'I would agree with that.' 'Therefore, is it true we could say, just as we cannot return to how things existed before, as yesterday is gone, that our measure of today must be by the accountability of our actions in determining whether we are leading a good or bad life? That in this knowledge, our soul may feel encouraged?'

'Dr Drakos, I presume?' spouted a short, fat man, interrupting Mikhael's train of thought and causing him to jump and take stock. 'Dr Hausen, it is a pleasure to meet you at last.' 'So, which are you? Dragon or ogre?' he laughed, not realising the truth behind the name. 'Some may call me an ogre if they bore of my knowledge of antiquities, such as this Black-Glazed Greek Lamp. Can you imagine what this lamp may have witnessed in the function of its role, what stories it could tell us of Plato, his mentor Socrates and the nighttime festivities which occurred privately behind the closed doors of the Andron?' 'Poppy cock, it would only tell us they were fools who questioned the glorious might of their nation, which ultimately caused its downfall!' Answered the doctor.

Immediately, Mikhael disliked this man. He had seen the same pompous attitude in many, who could never know for themselves the truth as they hadn't lived through it. Centuries ago, he would have tried to reason the truth out and encourage a better understanding, but now he had little taste for it. He had seen too many of his kind persecuted and executed by such men who had held power and acted above the law with little ability for reasoning. 'History does testify that each great nation eventually sees its own downfall; perhaps this is all part of an evolutionary cycle?' suggested Mikhael. 'Well, I think...' 'Shall we take a look at the Egyptian carved wood figure of Seneb?' he added quickly to shut the man up. His previous excitement ebbed away in despair as he guided the man around the exhibits, spending as little time as he could without being considered discourteous.

Afterwards, he sat quietly reading in his office. As he read his favourite line from 'The Solitary Stroller and the City', his soul shuddered and wept as the all-consuming darkness growing within him nodded. The line always spoke volumes to him; he was alone and felt out of place, out of time. Feelings deepened in his mind that his unnaturally long life was soon to end. He had felt it coming for years, deep inside, like a darkness eating away at him. Lately, each day, he had felt a little weaker. The afternoon dragged, and Mikhael tried to gain solace from the exhibits as usual, but this afternoon, they just stared back at him silently, keeping their stories to themselves.

Driving home during rush hour, he turned on the radio; they were playing what they called classic rock. He could never get used to others' ideas about what they considered old. Only in archaeology had he found like-minded individuals focused more on the ancient. 'Sunshine of Your Love' by Cream was playing, and the rhythmic throbbing of the music enthralled his senses; the guitar riffs spoke of hope to him in a way they never had before, not even when he had seen Cream Live back in 1967, their music had never before moved his soul in this way. The concert, he recalled with a smile creeping onto his face. He remembered how the considerable audience had reminded him of the time he had seen Antigone performed long ago in ancient Athens. There, from the safety of the tree line, which edged around the Theatre of Dionysus, he had seen the crowds, felt the excitement, and for a short time, his spirit had been enveloped in joy. As the song spoke to him, the once straight, precise edges of Mikhael's world seemed to blur into a new understanding. Daunted by these new feelings he pulled the car over at Mel's Drive-In, a restaurant he had driven past countless times. As his past blurred out of reality, he walked under the bright neon lights and up to the shiny counter and ordered a coffee. The restaurant was retro-styled to feel like 1950s America. As he sat drinking his coffee, he took in the vibe. The wall opposite him sported black and white images of their grand opening back in the day; every glance showed relics of a bygone age. He beckoned the waitress over with a backwards nod of his head. 'The owner must really miss the 50's?' 'Who Mel, Naa!' 'She sez it's part of who we are! Mel don't live in the past, but sure celebrates it!' 'Can I get you anything else? We do a mean Chilli burger, the best in town!' 'No, thanks, I'll just stick with the coffee!' the waitress smiled and turned her attention to another waiting customer. As the cup reached his lips, the jukebox sprung into life, attended by a skinny man who looked like he worked for the city, judging by his overalls and cap. Mikhael's senses were once more enthralled as the lyric, again, struck a chord deep inside, so deep his eyes misted as he listened intently. As the music engulfed Mikhael's emotions, he realised he had been blind; all this time, he had been agonising over a desire to return to a place long gone. However, now he finally understood the words of Socrates. He had been blind, 'today is just a progression of yesterday! This is where I belong with Francesca and Belinda', he realised. And with that realisation, the years of pain, the terrible things he had done and seen which had formed a life-sucking burden of darkness in his soul. A burden he had carried from one time to another, ever growing with each unnecessary act, was released. His exhaustion was gone, replaced with a glow of optimism he had not felt for centuries. This world was his, and the opportunities seemed endless; it even scared him a bit after so many years of looking backwards to now, once again focus on the future.

Grandmother's Chair

Fear gripped hold of his mind seeing his accuser again. She appeared on his screen, online in a pre-Family Court waiting room. She was a small, sickly, thin woman whose cold demeanour gave the appearance her life had seen no happiness. She, too, seemed anxious, shifting in her seat, periodically looking away from her screen.

Perhaps the guilt of her false allegations is etching into her conscience, he thought. He held no love nor forgiveness for this woman, as her actions had ripped all that he had loved away from him. No, Liam hated her, and seeing her face brought all his painful memories and heartache back to the surface. It was too much to deal with; he looked away from the screen and around the room where he stood. His surroundings were dark and dingy. Outside, rain clouds had engulfed the blue sky, and with it, most of the daylight had died away. The room was old-fashioned to his taste, yet everything represented home to Liam. As he flicked a light switch, an optimistic glow filled the room. Many details of the room stood out, from the butterfly paintings on the walls to the lesser-seen cracks (some of which had been painted over following a burst pipe many winters ago). So much had changed in Liam's life since his grandmother had passed away. He couldn't feel joy anymore; self-doubt and fear ran riot amongst his inner thoughts. 'I am cursed to lose everyone I love!', Liam thought.

The judge wasn't due to join for another ten minutes, so he crossed the room to the old rocking chair by the fire. It had been his grandmother's chair, and as he sat down, the fabrics released a waft of a strange pungent smell. It was a recognisable smell to Liam, but one that he just couldn't place. As the years had gone by, she had spent more and more of her time sitting there watching the world through the window, taking part in life more as a bystander than an active partaker. There had only been Liam and his daughter for company, but she had never complained.

Looking towards his laptop, sat upon the mahogany table he recalled his daughter's seventh birthday party and a feeling of joy mixed with his pain. Eliza loved butterflies, well, as much as she could love anything. The faintest hint of a smile was all that could be sought from her. Her entrance into this world had been traumatic. A challenging early labour had left her with brain damage. His wife, Jane, had only been twenty-six weeks pregnant when, just like his parents, the family curse wrenched his beloved wife out of his arms and out of life.

Eliza's cake had been shaped like a butterfly. Her eyes had glimmered with excitement when he'd walked up to her wheelchair holding the lit cake singing, 'Happy Birthday'. Tears formed in his eyes now as the momentary feeling of joy turned again to loss. He remembered how that night, when, after the guests had left and he had carried Eliza to bed, she had become upset and frustrated with herself and the condition that left her so isolated. His Grandmother had calmed her, making her smile again with her kind words and beautiful stories about butterflies. She had finished by saying, 'Life is like a butterfly; you go through changes that seem impossible and then along comes something beautiful'. They were words Liam knew well from his grandmother, words she had spoken to him countless times as he grew up in her care.

Liam's nose and throat had grown sore, and he got up to fetch a drink from the kitchen. He routed through cupboards to find a can of pop, to no avail. He checked the pantry, but it only had out-of-date gardening chemicals stored there. His throat was getting quite sore by now and his eyes were joining in sympathy. This sudden onset of illness left Liam feeling giddy and unwell. He gave up his search and accepted tap water, which he enjoyed much to his surprise, as it eased his sore throat so well. With his symptoms eased, he returned to the front room and re-took his seat, again wafting high the smell from the chair's fabric. In short time, Liam felt his nose begin to run, so he grabbed a tissue from his pocket. After wiping his nose, he looked and, in horror, found a red, blood-stained tissue. He realised it was a nosebleed. His mind tumbled backwards over all that had passed, over all his losses, back to the family curse.

'I was fine before', he thought, 'until I smelt...' The foundations of his whole life began to shake and crack. 'It's Grandmother's weed killer!' He stood up as quickly as he could, with his mind racing across time and past events. His chest was growing tight, and his breathing became so hard now that his legs buckled and gave out from below him. He tumbled and fell forward, crashing into the floor. In his weakened state, the cold, hard wooden floor felt unreal against his face. He thought about Eliza and focused on his arm muscles as he pushed against the floor, trying with all his might to get up, but his effort was in vain as all strength eluded him, and his arm flopped out across the floor. He thought about the curse, about so many deaths, his parents, uncles and aunts, even his beloved Jane, and how they had all suffered from nose bleeds before they had died.

"Why Grandma, why?" Liam mouthed weakly, all alone in the empty house as his vision dimmed and he slipped into an unconscious state.

As Liam lay unconscious and barely holding on to life, a solitary voice called out to him from the laptop sitting on the Mahogany table. It was Liam's nemesis, the social worker whom he so despised, "Mr. O'Connor, Mr. O'Connor, are you ok?"

"Liam, Liam", a soft voice spoke, a voice that spoke volumes, a voice he loved and had missed dearly. He opened his eyes and saw he was no longer lying face down on the hard wooden floor. In truth, he wasn't even in his grandmother's house anymore. Liam was lying on, well, he didn't know what he was lying on, but it looked like a white cloud! "Liam", the voice repeated, and he looked up into the eyes of his beloved Jane. A calmness filled Liam's body; he felt at peace with the world, feeling a deep happiness for the first time in an age. All fears and worries left him at that moment, replaced by a warm fuzzy feeling deep in his soul. He was with Jane; he was home. "Am I dead?", he asked. Jane smiled warmly, just as she always had and kissed Liam on his lips. She rested her forehead against his and whispered, "No, it is not your time, my love; you must go back and care for our Eliza!" With those words, his soul fell backwards into the harsh reality Liam's body faced.

Bright lights stung his eyes as he struggled to open them. When he finally managed to, shapes slowly came into focus. He realised Jane was gone and he was in hospital breathing through a noisy ventilator. His throat was dry and raw, and his chest shook and felt as if it was on fire, stinging with every vibration from the machine. He tried hard but couldn't move. "Hello, Liam; glad to see you're awake. I'm Nurse Wendy; I am taking care of you today." Liam tried to talk and managed a gargling noise before falling into a choking fit, which set off alarms on the ventilator. The nurse used a suction straw and eased Liam's choking, "Now don't worry, Liam, you are doing well, but you can't speak because the doctor has given you a drug to keep you paralysed whilst the ventilator helps your lungs. The doctor will be in to see you soon; he is doing his rounds and will be able to explain everything better." In hearing the soothing voice of the nurse with her calming tones Liam relaxed a little and drifted off back to sleep.

Voices disturbed his dreams as he heard the nurse and the doctor speaking. "Well, he just woke up and tried to speak, doctor. I used some suction to ease his choking, and he drifted off soon after!" stated the nurse. "I see; he is a strong fellow, isn't he? Well, according to his notes, I think we can increase the dosage to keep him settled." Again, Liam tried to speak, wanting to ask the doctor questions, yet only managing a gargle followed by another fit of choking. "This is what he did before.", said nurse Wendy as she grabbed the suction straw and settled Liam again. "Everything is okay, Liam; remember I told you not to try and talk." The doctor moved forward into Liam's eyeline, "Hello, Liam, I am Doctor Adrian and can imagine you must have many questions, but as nurse Wendy just said, you really should not try and speak, as your body needs the ventilator to help you with breathing at the moment and every time you try and talk, you are effectively fighting against the ventilator. I am confident that you will be okay with little or no issue in the long run, but right now, you need to rest, so I am going to increase a drug to keep you more settled and comfortable. This will give your lungs the best ch ..." Liam heard no more as he drifted back to sleep.

Days passed by, and Liam slept in an induced coma, briefly waking at times when the drugs started to wear off. He caught glimpses of faces and heard a few words here and there before slipping back into his world of dreams. He dreamt often about Eliza; he dreamt she was crying and being comforted by that social worker. He dreamt about Jane too, and she told him everything would be okay.

Liam came to slowly, the room was quiet. Not silent, but quieter than usual, which felt a little unnerving. He opened his eyes and saw the nurse sitting at her table, she was writing in his notes. Tilting his head slightly, he saw the ventilator was gone, which meant only one thing: he was breathing on his own; his lungs must have healed. "Eliza!", a voice whispered in his mind. Slowly moving his head to his right, he saw Eliza sitting, asleep in her wheelchair. She was holding his right hand. He could barely move but forced every ounce of energy into that hand and gently tightened his grip as a tear of joy escaped his eye and ran down his cheek.

A woman came into view, standing behind Eliza. Her face was familiar, but it took a moment for Liam's scattered thoughts to place it. It was Eliza's social worker. "Mr O'Connor, it is good to see you are doing so well; we had all been frightfully worried when you collapsed. Eliza was insistent that she saw you and very keen to stay by your side; she wouldn't have it any other way.", she said with a caring smile. "It has been decided that you will see Eliza every day whilst you are here, and we will look to sort something similar out for you both once you're well enough to go home." Liam's eyes watered with raw emotion; he was getting his daughter back into his life. Jane had been right.

Splintered Worlds

I sat still, hardly acknowledging what else the judge said. I had lost; my children had lost! They would be going into two separate foster families in the neighbouring town of Elksville, away from the home they knew and loved. I didn't feel like my usual positive self, but lost instead, in a deep void of despair and darkness. 'This can't be happening!', I thought, praying I would wake from the nightmare that had become my life. In front of me, the courtroom occupants, the barristers, solicitors and social workers started packing away their files. The judge had left. This case was over for them; they would walk away with their lives unaffected. They could now return to their everyday lives without any intense feelings of gloom. One by one, they moved towards the exit. It seemed that only I cared. Only I, the neglectful parent, truly cared about my kids' well-being and happiness. My hopes had been crushed, and as I moved now, my body felt sluggish, almost detached from my mind. I moved like an empty vessel amongst the tide of legal bodies.

Once outside and in my truck, I sat alone and stared blankly as the rest of the world carried on with business. I knew it wasn't the case, but it felt like everyone had turned their backs on me, my peers at the university, the forestry commission, and now, social services had targeted my family. I felt insignificant, almost invisible. My will to live was draining from me. Darkness now clouded my mind and desiccated my soul. It was late in the afternoon, and the schools were emptying out. Mothers walked by on their way home, laughing and playing with their sons and daughters. A painful reminder of a small joy I would no longer be able to experience. I steadied my shaking hand and lit a smoke to try and settle my mind and hold back the flood of tears I could feel. Men do not cry! My instincts yelled, but men do, of course, and I did. As I sat there isolated, downtrodden and heartbroken, I cried my eyes out, unable to stem the flow of tears. I struggled to come to terms with the pain. How can such trauma be accepted? Knowing my beautiful children had been taken away, I struggled to find the strength to carry on; there seemed no point.

It was true that I had been absorbed in my research on deforestation consequences for the past few months. However, I had done everything in my power to care for my kids. How could they accuse me of negligent parenting because Ann had been late to two dental appointments? Sure, I had been half an hour late picking both Ann and Nick up from school one Friday afternoon, but surely, if they understood the vital importance of my work, then they would see everything from a different perspective. I had been as honest as I could recall and tried to show them the truth of the matter, having shared the basics of my research. It had done no good and only provided the so-called social workers something to amuse themselves with, as they smirked at each other as I spoke up in front of the judge (a man I had assumed would be well-educated). During the break, I had even abandoned my science-based logic and prayed to God for help. However, no guiding hand of God nor any mystical force beyond our understanding cared sufficiently to help. Society, friends and God ousted me from their love and support, so, along with my children, I had been cast out upon a perilous journey into the unknown.

My wife had not attended court today, or any day previously. Having been lost to us in a coma for the last eight months, following a car crash. Yet the judge granted no adjournment, no consideration for a family going through a difficult time. This supposedly educated man provided no consideration for the existence of a struggling mother... how could you remove children without hearing a mother's oral statement! Where was the justice?

I was filled with despair. I envisioned a future where my beautiful Louisa woke from her coma, only for me to tell her how devastated our lives had become. How could I possibly break the news to my wife that we had lost our children? How could I convey this without destroying her spirit? Without robbing her of the strength she needed to recover. Without extinguishing her will to live. I already felt the emptiness calling to me, and I knew it would call to her as well.

During my preparations for the court case, I sought logic and compassion that could support our argument. I came across accounts of mothers and fathers who had died shortly after receiving such court orders, with some even suffering heart attacks on the courthouse steps. "If they were not good parents, why would their hearts give out on them?" I had wondered. I wondered no longer; I knew the answer. They were good parents, but our society held a blind acceptance of this country's draconian application of family law, a law that existed without compassion.

After an hour in despair, putting off the inevitable, I realised that I couldn't change what had happened. I had to accept my loss in its most painful form and move on. So, I started the engine and headed home. As I drove alone, in the quiet and solitude of the countryside roads and lanes, I felt the intense pull from the void to allow my truck to slip off the road, over the main bridge or into a wall.

In the days that followed, I avoided work. I simply couldn't face going back to the research that had taken precedence in my life. Not now that I felt such loss. One day, the weight on my soul became too much. I had been drinking all afternoon and couldn't carry the pain any longer. I had been worn down, told that I was a terrible parent and should not be allowed to have children. As I looked in the rear-view mirror of my truck, the man I saw looking back at me was a stranger, not me. It was someone I did not recognise any more. My soul screamed out for peace, for the endless torment to cease. I drove the six miles to the river. Here, everything made sense. Upon the bridge, I looked down and felt the urge, the call of the white waters below. This was how I could grant my soul rest. One more step was all it would take! An end to my personal despair. The river ran fast below me as I stood upon the bridge, a monument to all those many lives that had ended here through similar circumstances. Upon its highest point, I had stopped and stared down into the abyss, feeling the pull beckoning me. Strong eddies would pull anything and anyone straight under here if my body missed the rocks below the one-hundred-foot drop, that is. Chances of survival would be slim. After all, if I were doing this, I would do it right. I waited, running over everything again in my mind, 'was there any feeling of hope in me? Did I have any worth?', the answer came back, 'NO!' I stepped up onto the rails, this was it, my final moment on this wretched planet, I had decided.

I looked up from the fast-moving waters as it occurred to me that the river waters were higher than normal today. As I looked up, I could see the town of Elksville next to the river. "Our children are there, I thought!" Then, past the town, was the Forest of Elk, where I had been studying the effects of deforestation. Hardly any of the previously huge forest was remaining, thanks to the lumber companies who had cut down vast areas of the forest, like a corporate scourge. In only three years, they had wiped out so much of the forest that what was left was barely sufficient to stabilise the great hillside.

I had warned the Forestry Commission about this, time and time again, over the last year, but no one seemed to care. The truth was that the council received huge taxes from the lumber companies and had relaxed the laws to keep the money rolling in. 'Give up!' ran through my mind, and my eyes were drawn back to the beckoning river below. I lifted my right foot from the railing and leaned forward! All I could hear was the raging waters below; nature's cleansing power awaited me. I closed my eyes and, for some reason, hesitated. Perhaps it was the last ebbs of a strong survivalist instinct within me, or perhaps it was God. I don't know, but just before I took that final step, I waited. 'Buzz buzz buzz', The vibration of my mobile startled me, nearly causing me to leap off the bridge in fear as my phone interrupted the peaceful beckoning call of nature. After regaining my senses, I took out my phone; it was Child Services. I ignored the call and put my phone away. I looked out upon the forest once more and noticed something new. There was smoke coming from what was left of the old forest. The smoke was growing in intensity, signalling that a forest fire had broken out. My mind joined the dots using my knowledge to fill in the blanks. Estimating the damage this fire was doing to the last remnants of the forest. Then, considering how high the river currently was, it all meant one thing: the last few days of heavy rainfall had saturated the local water table. I focused harder on the mountainside, beside the town of Elksville, and my eyes widened with fear. The whole mountainside is going to destabilise and come crashing down on the town. Thoughts of Nick and Ann being caught up in the disaster raced through my mind, and I leapt over the railing and ran towards my truck. I had to get to them, but I didn't know where exactly they lived now, just that it was in the town. Child services rang my phone again, this time I answered in earnest, "Where are Nick and Ann? I need to know, it's urgent!" I demanded. Taken aback somewhat with the forthright demand from me, the social worker stuttered, "B, b," B, b, but, Mr Adam, I have been trying to get hold of you, concerning your children. They are on a trip to the gold mining museum in the Forest of Elk, but were due back two hours ago, and we can't get hold of them!" "They are in the fire!" I spoke without even realising I had voiced my concerns. "I am sorry, Mr Adams; I will ring you as soon as I hear anything more. We have notified the police, and they are ..." The conversation ended abruptly as I hung up and drove off towards the mountain. As I was driving, I called the sheriff's office and warned them to evacuate the town. They responded that they would send some officers to investigate my claims. I took the long mountain road that skirted the edge of town, the ground was more rock than soil there, and I knew it would not give way beneath me. As I neared the museum, smoke hung thick in the air and found its way into the truck, stinging my eyes and making driving harder than ever. As I reached the museum, I found it void of life. Clearly, everyone had fled back down the mountainside towards the false sense of safety they felt in town. After scouring the museum for any hint of life, I got back in my truck and pulled up the array of GPS motion trackers I had installed all along the forest two years ago, when I had started my deforestation research.

Devils' Slope lay directly ahead and would be the most lethal part of the mountainside. Once the collapse starts, Devils Slope, with its clay-like under soil, would just become a giant slipway for the topsoil, especially now that all the lower-lying trees had been cut down. The sensors showed no movement yet, but Neil knew he couldn't take his truck any further, for fear of the weight being the catalyst the area was waiting for. So, with his heart racing, he pushed on by foot into the smoke-choked forest, with nothing but a backpack, a map and his sensors to guide him. The acrid scent of burning trees stung his nostrils and eyes as he walked. Desperation fuelled his every step, driving him forward through the inferno that threatened to consume everything in its path. His children's faces flashed in his mind, their scared faces and imagined cries echoed in his ears, spurring him on despite the overwhelming odds. The professor saw light glinting from ahead, and he ran towards it in the hope of finding the coach and his beloved Nick and Ann. As he neared the flashing light, he saw it was not the coach and found that he had stumbled over the wreckage of a crashed plane, which contained the charred remains of its pilot. In an instant, he realised, the downed plane had caused the forest fire. He knew there was little time to be had and marched forward down the trail used by cars and coaches alike. They had to be here somewhere, he thought as hope carried him on.

Each obstacle he faced seemed insurmountable: the encroaching flames, the collapsing trees, the somewhat unstable ground beneath his feet. But Neil knew he must carry on for his children. An opening in the burning forest allowed him to glimpse what must be the back end of the coach. Thankfully, the coach rested, unscathed, a good way past the fire line in an opening. As the professor neared, a new predicament came clearly into focus. The trail had collapsed, trapping everyone inside with the fear of falling down the mountainside if the ground gave way any further. He knew the efforts of all aboard to remain still held little sway with the landscape the coach was poised upon, he had to move fast. Frantically pulling at the rear door, it soon became obvious it would not open; a dent halfway down, presumably from a falling tree, had jammed it tight. The only safe way out would be through the big rear window. The noise he had made, whilst fruitlessly grappling with the rear door, had stirred the children trapped fearfully inside into renewed panic and motion, which caused the coach to shift slightly, creaking upon its tired suspension. "Stay still! It's okay! Stay still!" Neil shouted out to the children in the hope of calming their movements. "Stay calm, don't move, I am going to try and get you out!", "Dad!" two instantly recognisable voices shouted back amongst the panic within. "Is it you, Dad?" shouted Ann. "Yes, Ann, it's me, don't worry, I will get you out, keep still, stay calm!". Neil rummaged through his backpack, retrieving a small axe. "Cover your faces with your hands, I am going to break this back window!" He took off his jacket as he gave the children a moment to follow his instructions. Looking into the coach, the professor could see the children all sitting bent forward in crash positions, protecting their faces. "Okay, I am going to smash the window now!" he shouted, allowing the children to brace their already fragile nerves. He held his jacket between his face and the window as he swung - CRASH! Went the window with one blow from the axe. Neil then quickly used the axe to knock away small, jagged pieces of glass that jutted up from the frame and put his jacket over what was left. "Everyone must remain still and calm!" he warned. "I will ask you one by one to move to the back and climb out. We have to take this slowly. Do you understand?" he asked. An unambiguous "Yes" was returned.

"Okay, one person from the front of the coach, please stand up slowly and walk towards the back". The first person was not a child, but a woman, who soon became visible as the social worker who had taken away his kids! "Climb out slowly", he warned her. Next was a child, then another, and another. It all went well until Emma, a young girl of six, tripped over a fallen bag inside the coach. She sprained her ankle, and even once every occupant was safely outside of the coach, Neil knew Emma would struggle to keep up with the group. Looking into the coach for any stragglers, Neil saw the driver remained, slumped over the steering wheel. He looked towards Wendy Jones, the social worker and asked, "The driver?" Not a single word left the lips of Wendy, but a shake of the head told Neil all he needed to know. The driver was dead. With fifteen children now standing in the opening, Neil realised he had more to do than just save his family. Everyone now looked to him for support, even the social worker he despised. Neil reached out to pick up his jacket as a tremor shook the ground, which immediately gave way beneath the coach amongst the screams of the children as twenty tonnes of metal disappeared, out of view, crashing down the mountainside. "Get back to the tree line!" shouted Neil as he stepped back himself. Everyone ran over to the trees in a panic. Everything was quiet apart from the splintering and crackling of trees twenty-five meters to the right. With his sensor array display in hand, Neil studied the data, before announcing, "We are best moving higher up the mountainside! We need to get up past Angel's rock! Up there, the land is pediment, that means solid bedrock! Up there, we will be safe!" Ann and Nick hugged their father and Neil vowed never to leave their sides again. The social worker bit her tongue and kept her displeasing thoughts about Neil's vow to herself; after all, she did owe Neil her life. Before they all moved off up, the professor radioed in that he had the children and they were all moving up the mountain, using the emergency channel on his walkie-talkie. The plan was formed that mountain rescue would airlift them from Angel's Rock, once they got there. They had been making slow progress, up through the old forest of the mountain, when an alarm sounded from the professor's backpack. "Everyone, stop for a minute.", he ordered as he investigated the strange alarm. The fire below them had spread, now engulfing the path behind which they had walked. "That's odd!" he spoke out loud as he looked at the screen of his sensor array display. "What's wrong, Dad?" asked Ann, as the whole group suddenly grew worried that a fresh concern was on its way! "My sensors all show a shift of several inches!" he exclaimed, standing up and looking across the mountainside for answers. "This just doesn't make any sense! The sensors can't all move at the same time!" he paused for a moment, studying the outline of distant mountain tops, "Unless...". "What, what is it, Dad?" Nick begged. "Unless..., this mountain we are on is situated under a magma chamber!" Hearing Neils' words, Wendy's eyes widened, "We are on a volcano!" she spluttered in disbelief. "That can't be, there are no volcanoes near here!" she continued. "There is no other answer; this mountain must be sitting upon an ancient magma chamber, and the pressure is building under us! ... That is why the sensors all show a movement of several inches. The magma chamber is swelling!" retorted Neil, who spoke, caught up in a trance, as his mind considered what awful events were about to plague their escape from the mountain. Grabbing the walkie-talkie out of his backpack, he radioed in on the emergency channel again, "This is Professor Neil Adams, calling from Mount Carla. I need you to call off the mountain rescue! New data shows the mountain is on top of a magma chamber and is about to blow. Mount Clara is about to become a volcano, and you need to evacuate the town of Elksville immediately!" The children cried in fear, hearing his words and the social worker tried to settle them, telling them they would be okay. The radio responded, "How can you be sure of this, all we have seen are a few landslides?" Turning away from the upset children and talking in a quieter voice, the professor spoke, "You have only seen the first signs. I have sensors all over this mountainside, and all of them show a shift upwards of several inches. That only happens when pressure builds in a magma chamber below; there is no other explanation! We may have hours or even minutes, I can't say; however, if you ignore my warning now, no one in the town of Elksville will survive this day! Evacuate the town now, we are going to find our own way off this mountain today, over and out!" The professor turned off the walkie talkie and turned to the scared group and paused for a second as he considered the terror of the situation, they found themselves stuck in. "We have quite a task ahead of us, and I am not going to lie to you, the going will be hard. However, I promise you all that we are going to find our way off this mountain!", he looked around, searching for landmarks and the safest route off the mountainside. As he stood, he felt the wind brushing against his face and instantly felt the immediate danger. "Right now, we are directly in the path of any pyroclastic flow or lava that will come off the mountain, when it blows." The professor pointed up at the top of the mountain and continued, "If we take note of how steep the mountain top is directly above us, compared to either side, we can see there is a high chance that when the volcano erupts, the lava will take the easiest path down the mountain, and we are on that path!" "What are you saying professor?", asked Wendy, who was clearly as terrified as the kids. "What I am saying is, that we need to get over there." Neil pointed over to the right of the mountainside where a steep ridge jutted out, "If we can get there, we will be safe from any immediate ash or lava flow! That is where we need to go." "That's impossible, it is at least three miles away and there is no way we can climb that!", answered the fear filled social worker. "If we are going to survive today, then we will make it!", the outburst of the social worker had done nothing to settle the fears of the children and Neil focused now on the children, "There is no-one who knows this mountainside as well as me, I have spent years studying this forest. Trust me, when I say we can do this, and do this we shall. Now, I will carry Emma and lead the way. Miss Jones, you will stay at the rear, and we all will walk off this mountain!" With that, Neil handed his son, Nick, the backpack to carry and picked up Emma. "Come on, we don't have time to waste!"

The trek was tiring and hard going for the younger legs in the group. Half an hour passed, and the group was only halfway to their goal when the earth tremors began. The girls screamed, and some lost their footing and fell over. Neil looked into the far distance, where the town sat beneath the mountain as sirens sounded. 'Now they believe me!', he thought. "Don't panic, this is just a warning from the mountain. We still have time." He helped those near him who had fallen over back to their feet as he spoke, "Let's pick up the pace, just to be sure." With that, the group moved on, a little faster than before. As they reached the ridge, the group took to scrambling up the steep side as the ground shook and shook with deeper intensity. Moments from the top, a deathly silence covered the mountainside. The tremors stopped, and all went quiet as if every creature held its breath. It was the silence before the storm, and moments later, thousands of birds filled the air, all desperately escaping the clutches of the soon-to-be fiery volcano upon which the group stood. Without warning, the tremors returned, growing stronger than ever with every second that passed, and the group all fell to the ground where they stood. Then, high above them, there was an almighty bang, and as members of the group tried to regain their footing, a shockwave blew them back to the ground amongst falling trees. "Stay down, take cover against the rocks!" shouted Neil as the volcano blew its top and chunks of rock began bombing the ground. The ground started to shake once more amidst the cries and screams of the children. "We need to move now, get to your feet. Come on, we are nearly there!" shouted the professor as the aerial assault had ended. Moving was hard, and the group had to clamber over the fallen trees, blown down by the shock wave. Ann was at the back of the group with the social worker, Wendy, when it happened. Alerted by his daughter's call, Neil turned around to see his daughter slip down out of sight where she stood! With his heart racing, he put Emma down and stumbled past the group to where she had stood. The grim reality struck his eyes, and a panic grew in his soul as he saw his daughter and Wendy both clutching a fallen tree as they dangled above a lake of lava. The ground had opened beneath them, and now they both screamed in pain as their legs felt the heat. Seconds later, Neil was hanging over the edge, holding on to Ann with one hand and Miss Jones with the other. "I can't pull you up! You need to climb up me!" he ordered. Ann listened and followed her father's instruction and reached and pulled herself up as much as she could, reaching his shoulder before the earth shook once more, causing the tree to dislodge and fall into the lava. The social worker screamed as a splash of lava hit her legs, causing immense burning pain. "You need to climb!" he repeated, but the social worker just held on and screamed. He could feel his grip slipping, when another tremor saw his daughter slip. Without thinking, acting purely on a father's instinct, Neil caught Ann with both hands, stopping her fall. But, in doing so, he inadvertently let go of the social worker, Miss Jones, who released a tortured scream as she fell. Her cries of fear and pain were silenced only as the lava devoured her body. However, there was no time for remorse as the lava surged upwards. Neil pulled his daughter to safety, and the whole group made a renewed effort to scramble up the last fifty meters of the ridge.

Sat, catching their breath on top of the ridge, the group could see smoke rolling down the mountainside. It was a pyroclastic flow, as the professor had predicted; it ran straight down the mountainside and avoided the ridge. The sky grew dark, and lightning struck all over the mountain as the tremendous force of the eruption ignited the very air into action. "We have bought ourselves a little time, but we can't stay here; we need to move on and head back down to the gold mining museum, where my pick-up is parked. That is our ticket off this mountain!" Seconds later, the group was back on their feet, and Neil was again carrying Emma as they continued along the ridge, high above the forest fire below. Every now and then, the great shaking of the mountain would cause them to stumble and fall. But they carried on, for the most part, uninjured, through the fading daylight, as ash fell all around them and blocked out the sunlight. With all that had been witnessed, every tremor generated great fear within the children, as they expected the earth to open up and swallow them, just as it had with Miss Jones.

Below them sat the gold mining museum, and they started their descent. They had crossed high above the forest fire below, yet now, the trees above were catching alight from the heat of the eruption, and even the ground where they walked started to smoke as the soil grew drier and drier. By the time the group reached the truck, visibility had reduced to only a few feet. It was only when everyone clambered into and onto the pick-up truck that one of the girls noticed her friend Samantha was missing. "Sam's not here!" she exclaimed, catching the professor's attention. After a quick check, Neil found that Samantha was indeed missing, and the others hadn't seen her for at least ten minutes. After considering the dire circumstances they faced, Neil announced, "I will retrace our steps for ten minutes to see if I can find Sam!" He turned to Nick whilst pulling out a flare gun, "Nick, I want you to wait fifteen minutes and then point this flare gun directly above you and pull the trigger! This will help me find my way back to you." Nick looked worried as he looked at his dad, "What happens if you don't come back?" "I promise you, I will be back; we are all getting off this mountain together! But, whatever happens, you all need to stay together, no one is to wander off on their own, is that understood?" "Yes, sir", the scared children answered. "Okay, I will be as quick as I can. Don't forget, fifteen minutes and then fire a flare straight up!"

Neil felt he was putting the lives of all the children at risk by taking this extra time to search for Sam. He wanted to get in that truck and drive his children away from the mountain, away from all the danger. In fact, it had been that single thought which had made him decide to search for Sam. If Ann or Nick were lost, he would just about sacrifice anything or anyone to find them, so he knew he just had to do right by Sam, too. As he stumbled and crawled, feeling the near blind path in front of him with his fingers for any signs of Sam, he called out "Samantha, Samantha". Over and over, he called, despite the thick, hot air scorching his dry throat as he called out. As he hit a particularly bushy patch of forest, he heard a faint reply amongst the rumbling and growling of Mother Nature's latest creation. "Help!" The call was faint but came from the right. Moving further right, Neil called out again, "I can hear you, Samantha! Keep shouting out to me!", "Help!" This time, the sound was very close, and he started feeling the ground again with his hands. "I am right here, where are you?" He called out again. A hand reached out to him, and Samantha was found. She explained that she had fallen and hurt her leg, but by the time she had got up, everyone had gone, so she sat still. "You did the right thing, Samantha. I have got you now, let us make our way to the others and get out of here!" However, finding their way anywhere would not be easy, there was no path that could be seen and every bit of ground felt like any other bit of ground. They had to head down slowly until the ground cleared and they reached level ground. He held Sam's hand tightly and slowly guided them down the slope. After a while, it felt like they had been travelling in circles. Neil reckoned they should have reached the truck by now, and yet, he was still to find the level ground of the trail he had driven on and felt rather lost. Then he heard a shot fired, and through the thick fog of ash, a red light soared up twenty meters or so to the left. Without any thought, Neil pulled Samantha toward the flare's light. "We are nearly there!" he assured her. Back at the truck, Neil realised he had crossed behind the museum and somewhere had been completely turned around in the dark. After helping Sam onto the back of the pick-up truck and giving Nick a thankful hug, he turned over the engine, and it fired up the first time. With all the lights on, they could see a couple of meters ahead of the truck. They crept back along the trail gently until gradually the daylight returned, and the group of survivors made it safely away from under the shadow of the volcano. Each of them looked identical, all covered in ash; they truly looked like survivors from a dystopian future. The world felt unreal and abstract to the group as they sat silently, dumbstruck from all they had just experienced. A military helicopter flew overhead when they were about ten miles away from the volcano, and they knew their ordeal was over.

Quantum Mania

Little did Nelson know what destiny had planned for him as he installed yet another lamp in his bedroom. His father was against his private war upon the dark, telling his son to "Grow up", that he was too old to sleep with the lights on!" However, Nelson didn't harbour any negative feelings towards his dad, for he knew his dad had never been in the same situation and simply would never be able to appreciate the full-on fear that gripped his mind and turned his soul to a shade of white each night as the light faded. "Dinner's ready!" The words invaded his thoughts, causing the hairs on the back of his neck to stand up on end, like an army of soldiers standing to attention, ready to receive orders before the battle. Soon it will start, thought Nelson. With depressed movements, he got up and made his way downstairs to the kitchen table. Nelson subconsciously hoped that in moving slowly, he would affect time itself, to somehow slow it down and even halt time at that precise moment. How he longed to be frozen in time, caught in a thrilling moment where the future stood still, sparing him from the impending hours of exhilarating terror that loomed ahead! Mid-meal, he found temporary relief as his sense of taste distracted his tired and fearful body from what may lie ahead. His mother's cooking was out of this world and certainly on a par with any top chef you could name. Worried about Nelson, his mum made every effort to get him to eat so he would have some energy to carry on living. This innate love and care came out in her cooking. Nelson loved his mum's food, and as he enjoyed the spaghetti and meatballs on his plate, for a few brief moments, he forgot his troubles and slipped into another state, the state of a happy thirteen-year-old boy. His mum smiled as his face developed emotions other than sadness, and as his eyes sparkled with fresh life, a tear ran down her face, which she wiped away before it could be seen.

After dinner, Nelson helped his mum to clear the table and placed the dishes in the dishwasher. The blind was down on the kitchen window already. This was something his mother did to help Nelson, for after dinner, it would start to go dark out, and his mum did everything she could to ease his troubles. Nelson stood in silence, staring at the blind and mentally questioning what existed on the other side of it. Rumblings, like murmurs, already existed, and he was grateful for the buzz being emitted from the kitchen light; it drowned out the sounds around him. Sounds that came from everywhere, but nowhere. Suddenly, he felt a presence behind him and jumped as he turned. It was his mum, "It's okay, Nelson, I've sorted your room ready for you, sweetheart." By this, she meant she had pulled his blind down and had closed his curtains, curtains which were joined together by Velcro to reduce any slim chance of accidental opening incidents. "Thanks, Mum", said Nelson, relieved for his mum's support and help. As he walked past, his mum gave him a cuddle and kissed him on his forehead, "Try and get some sleep, sweetheart, you need your rest." He answered as honestly as possible by giving a weak smile. As Nelson crossed the landing to his room, the light bulb which sat naked in its fitting grew brighter and then flickered intensely. A spew of distorted sounds entered his ears, the disjointed voices grew louder in relation to the flickering, until a loud scream caused Nelson to step back and nearly fall over Jessie, the family cat. "Is everything okay?" Mum shouted up the stairs as the flickering stopped. "Yes, everything's fine, Mum, I just had a sneeze!", "A sneeze! It sounded like a scream to me... but, so long as everything's ok, goodnight sweetheart." Nelson questioned if the scream he had heard had actually been his own. His mind boggled, he didn't think he had actually screamed, but he must have, at least, unless... his mum was starting to hear it too?

Nelson's room was lit up more than any room in the house, and as he closed his eyes that night, the noise being emitted from the desk lamps and the main light covered up every sound the dark held in store for him. Before he lay down to sleep, he prayed to God, "Please forgive my sins. Protect me from demons and keep my lights on." It was a prayer he said every night, and for just once, he hoped he would have a peaceful night's sleep. He hadn't slept for more than a couple of hours a night for as far back as he could remember. Poor Nelson constantly felt tired and struggled with school every day. His dad had said he would have to take him to the doctor if things didn't change, after Nelson's grades had dropped from A's to E's. He really didn't like that idea. Not wishing to tell anyone about his private issues and fears. There truly seemed to be no way forward for Nelson. If he did see a doctor and asked for help, he figured they would accuse him of having a mental illness and lock him up! If they did, then what would happen? If they locked him up and turned the lights off! The thought scared Nelson so much, he tried to push it out of his mind. Desperately trying to forget his worries, he thought about Wendy Miller, a girl from school whom he liked. He imagined walking along a sunny beach with her, hand in hand. Moments later, he relaxed a little, and his body gave in to the sleep he so desperately needed.

Nelson had known Wendy from their first day in nursery together; they had been inseparable. Wendy had never thought about Nelson as anything more than a friend, and then, when in high school, Wendy started going out with other boys, Nelson's heart broke in two. Not long after, his troubles began. Sleepless nights tormented him, and the pair drifted apart.

"Nelson", a quiet voice spoke gently, "Nelson, wake up!" the voice continued, "You're going to be late!" Nelson strained his eyes open, still half asleep, to see his mum leaning over him. Her lips moved, "Come on, wake up, Nelson", she said as his eyes gently closed again with the peaceful reassurance of her voice…" WAKE UP!" Nelson jumped awake to an empty room. He looked at the clock, it was 3.45 AM. Tonight had been a good night, he had slept for seven hours. Now he had to wait another two hours before the sunlight would keep him safe. He turned his TV on and streamed his favourite cartoon superhero, Professor Mindray! Nelson loved how the professor used his mind to manipulate and move objects in his continuing battle to defeat the villainous efforts of Zandor and the Army of the New Doctrine, whose every action was focused on enslaving the people of Earth. The lights in the room flickered several times, and Nelson felt his heart beat quicker as he feared they would go off completely. With every flicker, whispers of sentences invaded his ears!

"Dra gumpbri drain buwed!" and other unintelligible words flowed stronger on every flicker. It was always the same; the words never made any sense to Nelson. He knew too well that the invisible monsters of the night didn't speak English, and he could only imagine with great fear what they were plotting against him. What Nelson heard next sent him reeling in disbelief: "Hide from the Janus board!" It was English, or it certainly sounded like English at least! Was it a message? Was it a warning? What did it mean? "Hide from the Janus board!" Who was this Janus board? Nelson had never heard of them. And how exactly could he hide? It struck him that this warning may not actually be for him. For the first time ever, he considered that the voices he heard may not be intended for him. Perhaps he was just overhearing echoes of conversations from an invisible world! The fear he had always felt left suddenly as this new concept spun about the brain cells of his mind. Maybe he was not under attack! Perhaps, he had nothing to fear. However, he considered that just being able to hear the echoes from an invisible world was pretty damn scary on its own. If there is an invisible world, where is it? It can't be here, or we would know, we would bump into the invisible creatures. Unless…! A terrible thought sent chills down his spine once more. Unless they are spirits, ghostlike entities that exist in an afterlife that is controlled by this "Janus board"? Before he could contemplate further possibilities of the night's insights, the seven am buzz kicked in as the world jumped alive with daytime static. The static came from a waking world switching on kettles, radios and all sorts of phones and computers as people checked their social media accounts in their pre-work morning rituals. Along with the rest of the world, Nelson too, got up and dressed for the school day ahead. Nelson's mother was in the kitchen, just like every morning. And just like every morning, breakfast was waiting for him on the table. However, something was amiss. Something was out of place; the regular morning pattern was broken somehow, and Nelson spotted the issue almost straight away, and it made him feel uneasy! His mother looked different! She had not done her hair the same way she had always done before. Today, it looked a little straggly, like she had just got out of bed and left it. Nelson spoke, "Your hair! It's not right!" Taken back with concern, as if she had made the biggest faux pa possible, his mother looked away and in a useless attempt to fix the issue, stroked her hair with her hand, trying to put it into place, "It's ok Nelson, I will fix my hair now!" and with that she left the kitchen and returned moments later with her hair perfectly placed as it had been every morning before. Nelson liked patterns intensely; he saw patterns in everything. Mother having her hair done and being in the kitchen when he got up was part of a pattern that started every day for him. He closed his eyes and mentally went through his morning rituals again. He pictured himself getting out of bed, going to the bathroom, getting dressed, coming downstairs and into the kitchen, and then he opened his eyes... his mum was now part of the correct pattern. He took a deep breath, a sigh of relief, really, and then started on his breakfast. The texture of his cereal was slightly too soft, but he imagined it to be crunchy as he ate it. One change to the pattern was more than enough, so he would not even entertain the thought that his cereal had gone soggy. 'Crunch,' he thought as he ate every mouthful.

On the journey to school, he contemplated what had gone wrong today. Why had the pattern changed? He came up with two possible conclusions: either his mother was starting to become forgetful (but this didn't seem too likely as she was very much younger than his teacher, Mrs. Brentwood, and Mrs. Brentwood could remember so many academic facts that it seemed unlikely that old age could be a factor. The other, seemingly more likely possibility was that his mother had been disturbed during her sleep, waking later than usual, feeling tired and having left her hair in disarray to focus on her morning rituals. Yes, that made more sense, but then, what had disturbed her sleep? He remembered that his mother had heard a scream last night and wondered if she had started hearing the voices too. Had she heard about the Janus board when the lights had flickered? I'm overthinking again! He made a conscious effort to halt his train of thought. Instead, he stared blankly out of the window and tapped his thumb nervously against the wide expanse of empty seat beside him as his dad drove him to school. Everything seemed normal, children walked along, some with parents, some with older siblings, others with their friends. All were making their way to school. Cars were leaving driveways, and the postman's van was parked by the newsagents, as it normally was. Everything appeared to be normally summoning in just another regular school day. That was, at least, until three black vans drove past in the opposite direction. One black van would have been acceptable, but three black vans, one after another, were downright peculiar and did not fit in with Nelson's patterns. An uneasy feeling gripped him deep within. Today was not going to be a regular day. Today was going to stand out as downright different.

School seemed completely normal until lunch break, when from the cafeteria, he saw one of the black vans from earlier pull up alongside the school. He watched intently as the side door opened and a man in a black boiler suit and black cap got out and walked across the road to Lucy's Cafe. He returned a moment later with a sandwich and three coffees, indicating that there were at least three people in the van. The man took longer to get back into the van as he handed the sandwich and coffees to someone who remained out of sight inside. After that, he climbed back in, and the door closed. Those few moments he had taken getting in were enough for Nelson to take note of what looked like a wall of computer screens inside the van. His powerful mind exploded into thought. Having watched so many of those secret agent films that his father liked. Black vans with computers meant surveillance; it meant secret government agency work! All the dots aligned as Nelson saw the pattern converge in his mind... secret agency surveillance.... The breakfast abnormality and last night's otherworldly message. It all meant only one thing: he was not the only person who was receiving these messages or knew about the other world! That was all that he could conclude with the data currently available. Nelson was eager to take a look at the computer inside the van. He wanted to learn more and figure out if he was going crazy. For now, all he could do was carry on as if nothing unusual was happening and wait to see what would happen next.

The day continued like any other Friday. Nelson finished his lunch by himself, away from the other students, like he always did. Fore, he never enjoyed eating around others and prized his alone time at lunch. It was the only chance he had to be on his own at school, and he so badly needed this time to decompress after having to tolerate and be pleasant to the other students. He didn't think of himself as anti-social as such, I mean, he was pleasant to everyone, he just preferred his own company and found other people irritating. They would cough, sniff or even breathe too loudly and simply drive him potty. However, he would just smile and not say anything offensive to them, well, at least not out loud for them to hear. Internally, a host of curses and swear words would ruminate within Nelson's mind with every irritating noise he heard.

After lunch, a brief spark of interest grabbed his mind, when the Physics tutor, Mr. Underwood, made mention about the eleven-year cycle of solar flares and that today the worlds astronomers and satellite technicians were watching these flares carefully in fear of what destructive power such an increase may have upon the thousands of new satellites now orbiting Earth! Satellites which had not been orbiting eleven years ago, when the last flare-up climax caused many blackouts worldwide! Nelson, of course, lived in fear of blackouts and was on edge for the rest of the day. He didn't know why, but he did know the noise that accompanied electrical usage, the interference buzz, gave him peace from the other world. It seemed to sever the link to his mind, and if there was a black out! Well, Nelson just couldn't bear to think about that possibility.

At home time, Nelson spied the same black van parked around the corner from the school entrance. "What are they surveilling?" he thought to himself as his father drove them both home. The van seemed to follow them for a while before turning down another road and disappearing out of sight. At home, he sat slumped, exhausted, on the sofa in front of the television as he waited for tea to be ready. As he sat, waiting, he drifted off to sleep. The world about him was still abuzz with electrical interference, and he slept soundly. Having noticed he was fast asleep, his mother took a little longer to get tea ready, happy to see her tired boy get a little extra rest. She knew leaving tea too late would upset Nelson, so she woke him up for tea half an hour later than normal, and he barely noticed. Today had been an extremely trying day, but he felt a little refreshed from his nap and enjoyed his mum's cooking as always, which helped him to forget about all his woes for a little while. All went well until bedtime, when the unthinkable happened! Nelson was in the bathroom brushing his teeth when it began.

The bathroom light flickered, and disjointed, unintelligible whispers invaded his ears… "Ker…ba… wall.. ja… s DIE", Nelson dropped his toothbrush into the basin and took a step back as the flickering and voices both increased. Nelson's worst fears came true as he stood in a dark bathroom, feeling overwhelmed by the overlapping voices surrounding him. Fear gripped him, and he visibly started shaking, and tears welled up in his eyes. The voices were so clear, so real, he felt he could simply reach out a hand and touch them. With his eyes tightly closed, he faced his fear and reached out with his left hand first and then with his right. Stood in the dark of the bathroom, his fingers felt the faint outline of a woollen top, and Nelson took a deep breath and held it, frozen in fear. "SCRAGGILL!!" the voices yelled before suddenly being drowned out by a scream coming from downstairs that drew attention like a slap in the face. It was Mum, and he opened his eyes to find himself touching the towel rack. "Help!" his mum screamed, and he ran out of the bathroom and down the stairs instinctively despite the darkness. As he neared the bottom of the stairs, he saw a mixture of colours lighting up the walls of the lounge. "Help me!" his mother screamed as he rounded the corner to see her disappear in front of his eyes before he could reach her. Slipping through what could only be described as some kind of portal across space and time, she simply vanished in front of his eyes as the portal closed, and the room lit up with brilliant white lights from outside. Nelson looked towards the window to see where these lights came from. The front door burst open, and a team of military men, all dressed in black uniforms and wearing goggles, entered the house and surrounded Nelson and his dad! Nelson's father pushed against the agents entering the room, and they restrained him.

Without waiting, the men opened a large case they had carried in with them and removed a complicated-looking device, which they set upright on the floor. It had to be assumed they could see something with their goggles that was not visible to the naked eye, or at least that was what was going through

Nelson's mind as the men located the device exactly where his mother had vanished. "Turn on the Q.A.D., we need the insurgents' coordinates!" ordered one man, who must have been the team leader, as the men quickly turned on the device. The machine powered up with a screeching noise that overpowered Nelson's senses, and he dropped to his knees with his hands over his ears, trying to block out the painful screech. The room flickered with light as the intensity of the noise increased as the device reached its full capacity. And then, a shimmering sheen filled the space above the machine, like a doorway to another world. This machine had tapped into the realm beyond all that we knew to be true. Nelson gasped as he glimpsed his mother being pulled away by people across the divide. "That's my mum!" he shouted to the agents, "They've taken her!". The agents looked at each other before approaching Nelson. "Who has taken your mum, son?" He didn't know who they were; he just knew that they had. "They have!" he said, pointing across the divide. The image Nelson could see suddenly vanished as the device turned off. The Agents looked at each other again, as if they knew what Nelson was talking about. One of them spoke into his walkie talkie, "We have a stage two event and a QD here. Gateway protocol followed and co-ordinates retrieved." A single voice replied from the agent's walkie talkie, "Detain the QD!" The agent quickly spoke to Nelson, "It's okay son, you are safe, we will find your mum!" Then turning to Nelson's father, who had stopped struggling and was trying to just make sense of what had happened, the agent spoke reassuringly, "Sir, everything is under control, we are here to help", "You will both have to accompany us to base, we need to debrief you." "But my wife!", uttered Nelson's father. "Your wife has crossed over into another dimension, sir. We have taken measurements, and I assure you we will do all we can to retrieve her, but first you need to come with us!" The agents' words did not provide any level of comfort for either Nelson or his father, who both felt a massive part of their life had just left for good. Turning his attention to Nelson, who was crying and rocking back and forth on his knees, he cuddled his son, telling him it would all be ok. That his mother would be ok. He never for one second believed these words himself, but he knew, like any parent does, that sometimes, just sometimes, you have to fake confidence and tell a lie to ease your child's pain. "Come on, we have to get moving!" said the agent kindly, as his men ushered Nelson and his dad out of the house to the waiting convoy of black vans parked on the street. 'I knew today was going to be different!' was the thought that went through Nelson's mind as he saw the same black vans from earlier that day.

After a fairly long drive, Nelson and his father were taken to a plainly decorated room which had only a water cooler and a sofa in it. Here, without a single window or picture to break up the monotony, they were told to wait. An agent stood guard on the inside of the doorway, which definitely gave off the impression that they were captive and that there was no escape from whatever was about to come! Hours had passed before the main agent returned and asked them to accompany him to meet the base commander. Nelson was glad for the waiting to be over and happily went with him. They walked into an operations room, where agents sat in front of various computer screens, performing their jobs as ordered. "This is Nelson Harris, the boy I was telling you about, and his father, David Harris.", said the agent to the man in front of them, before turning to Nelson and his father and saying, "This is Commander Brennan; he is in charge of this facility." The commander shook the hand of Nelson's father, "Welcome to our facility Mr. Harris, I understand you must be struggling with everything you have experienced this evening, and I want to assure you that we are on your side and want to help get your wife," with a quick glance to Nelson, he continued, "and mother back!" "If you give me a moment, I will try to explain what has happened today!" "I would very much appreciate that, sir", responded Mr. Harris. "Bear with me, Mr. Harris, for this will sound quite extraordinary, for what has occurred is extraordinary... To begin with, you may have noticed that my men wore night vision goggles when you first saw them. These goggles are based on the differences seen in nocturnal animal eye structures when compared to those of humans. In cats, their visual systems are built differently from ours. Their pupils are three times larger than ours in the dark, which allows cats to capture the maximum of light available. Further to this, they have an additional layer of cells in their eye structure, which causes their eyes to reflect light and glow red or green at night."

"Our night vision goggles are based on their evolved technology. It was developed during the Second World War to allow military pilots to fly safely and spot targets at night."

"However, it was soon realised there existed a hitch with this technology. If I could ask you, Mr. Harris, do you recall ever seeing a cat staring into space blankly, as if it was watching something invisible?" "Well, I suppose I have seen cats behave like that at times, yes!" answered Mr. Harris. "Indeed, we have all seen cats act in such peculiar ways. During the war, it wasn't long before our pilots made strange reports of sightings, unexplainable sightings. Referring to having seen demons and the like! At the time, it was put down to exhaustion brought on by the long hours and insufferable conditions of the war!" The commander paused for a moment, letting that last bit of information soak in. "However, further testing has proved the existence of these visions! We can see levels of light, never before seen with these goggles, which even allow what we call quantum photons to become visible to the wearer. Quantum photons exist in our universe but have the ability to cross dimensions. When there is a surge of these photons, other worlds can become quantumly entangled with our own! They come and go, slipping in and out of our world. "Are they ghosts?" asked Nelson's dad, desperately trying to understand. "They are what I believe our culture has learnt to call ghosts. The very few who have been able to tune in to these quantum dimensions have felt they were being haunted, and it is only human instinct to fear what cannot be understood. We all do it and can all sense the dimensional slippage across our world to some extent. If you have ever felt chills down your spine on a hot day, or witnessed your hairs on your arms stand on end for no reason, then in the depths of your mind, you have likely sensed a quantum anomaly occurring around you!" "Is my mum in a quantum dimension then?" asked Nelson, who was following the commander's words with great interest and understanding. "Exactly right, Nelson. Your mother has somehow crossed over into another dimension. Now I am being one hundred percent open with you both, and I expect to receive the very same honesty in return. In fact, I will go as far as to say, I am depending upon your honesty and so is your mother!"

Nelson's father's eyes widened as the commander's line of questioning turned towards his son. His instinctive need to object and protect his son was just barely held back by his own need for answers. "Nelson", continued the commander, "Have you experienced any sensations that appear odd or otherworldly?" he had, after all, this was the vein of his life. At the same time, he saw visions of being studied and dissected by doctors and scientists if he honestly answered. He didn't speak, yet his silence spoke volumes to the commander. "I must admit, Nelson, that I do understand the fears you may have about disclosing such experiences. However, there is no need to fear telling me, you are safe here and no harm will come to you. By telling me, you will be helping your mother." Nelson wondered if he was safe, but he also knew his mother was gone, and he so wanted to help her. "Yes, I hear voices at nighttime, when everything is turned off!" "I knew it", said the commander with a glimpse of satisfaction. "Now tell me, Nelson, are you the only one who experiences this? Did your mother have the same gift?" "No, my mum never did. It was only me, every night." Nelson thought for a moment, remembering his mother's scream the other night and her bedraggled hair the following morning. "Well, she might have. I mean, the other night, she thought she heard me scream, and I didn't, I think she heard a scream from the other world!" The commander turned to Nelson's father, "Mr. Harris, please forgive me for asking these sensitive questions. You see, events such as these, which we call stage two events, usually occur around people sensitive to dimensional slippage. Now, we have the quantum coordinates of where your wife has travelled to. However, in order for us to be able to open a link to this dimension, we need more than just scientific data and calculations; merely knowing the coordinates does not open a portal." The commander looked momentarily at the floor, before looking back into Mr. Harris's eyes, "Quite frankly, we need Nelson to open the portal for us! Without him, we will not be able to establish a connection to retrieve your wife!" Nelson's mind was running amok with thoughts, the ultimate one which he eventually rested on was that he had to save his mum. "I will do it! I want to save MUM!" Mr. Harris's eyes opened wide with his son's statement. "I won't allow it!" he exclaimed. He approached Nelson and, whilst holding him by the shoulders, he explained his fears. "I can't let you do this, son. It is my job to protect you and keep you away from danger, not send you headfirst into it!" Secretly, he was thinking he couldn't bear losing Nelson as well as his wife. For if he lost his son, he would be alone in this universe! "But I have to do it, Dad! It is the only way to save Mum! It's what mum would want me to do!" "Your mum would want me to keep you safe, Nelson. Sorry, no, I can't allow this."

With them at an impasse that did not suit the commander's agenda, he piped in to restore a balance in his operational favour, "Your son would be quite safe, Mr. Harris. You can trust that my aim is not to endanger Nelson but simply retrieve your wife." After a short pause, he continued, "As you have seen, we have developed technology specifically aimed at tracking these events. Technology which has come out of many years of study. There is one such piece of technology which we call the Quantum Divergent Stabiliser. It is basically a wristband, which, when turned on, anchors the wearer within our dimension." The commander paused again, as if trying to reframe his words in his mind, "Provided Nelson is wearing an activated device, he will never suffer dimensional slippage like your wife, Mr. Harris" "You see, Dad, it's safe!", declared Nelson, making use of the commander's argument. It all sounded too fantastic to Nelson's Dad, and there was something he distrusted about the Commander, but he could hardly deny his son the chance to help with such assurances of safety abounding, "Ok, Nelson, you can help!" Nelson hugged his dad and smiled, feeling like the most unlikely hero. "Bring a Q.D. Stabiliser for this young man and run phase three protocols with the set of quantum coordinates retrieved.", instructed the commander to his team. It wasn't long before Nelson was next to the device that had been used at his home. This time, however,

Nelson was wearing a cap covered in electrodes, which were plugged into the device in the middle of the room, bathed in red light, which he felt symbolised an active mission status. Behind him to the right was a team of five agents. Once Nelson opened the portal, the agents would cross the divide and retrieve his mother. The agents were fully armed as they expected to meet with a fierce response. Nelson's father was not in the room but watching from behind a glass divide along with the commander and a team of technicians. He was deeply unhappy, having found out what the commander had been keeping to himself! Nelson was not to turn on his wrist device until he had opened the portal! "Initiate the process!" ordered the commander. The technicians leapt into action, confirming everything from the machine's status to the temperature of the room to each other as they worked through the portal creation protocols. The commander leaned forward and spoke into a microphone that was connected to the portal room, "Nelson, you will shortly hear the device start up. It will take a few moments to reach full power, and when it does, you will feel a strong pull to the other dimension. If all goes to plan, your abilities will allow the device to open a gateway to the dimension. Remember, once the red light turns green, it means the portal has been stabilised and you need to turn on your wrist device immediately, to avoid disrupting the portal." Nelson looked behind him at the commander, who stood safe behind the glass. "Did you get that, Nelson? Once the red light turns green, turn on your wrist device!", continued the commander. Nelson nodded, catching a glimpse of his father behind the commander. Nelson felt afraid, alone, but knew he just had to do anything he could to save his mum. The device powered up, and Nelson felt his mind being invaded by it. It felt as if the room was shaking as the device hummed louder and louder. He focused on his wrist; there was only one button on the device. Having jumped slightly as smoke billowed out of the device next to him, the commander spoke again. "That is just the cooling process, Nelson, nothing to worry about!" His focus blurred, and he began to lose touch with the reality around him. The device probed his brain, stimulating the parts connected to quantum manipulation. 'The light is still red!' he thought as he struggled to track his own reality. Lights buzzed across the room as the device threw up a portal, slicing across dimensions. Nelson stared ahead as his mother appeared in front of his senses once more. She reached out an arm to Nelson as their eyes met. Nelson felt faint but reached out in an instinctive response to hold his mum as everything turned dark and he fell to the ground. He hadn't turned on his wrist device; he hadn't even seen the light turn green, but as he hit the ground, the button was struck and the wrist device activated.

Nelson lay unconscious for a week. His brain had been stimulated to a point beyond what it could accept, and this had induced an internal shutdown, leaving him in a coma. As he came to his senses, he heard his mother's voice, "Everything will be ok, Nelson." He smiled, knowing he had helped save his mother; the plan had worked. He tried to open his eyes, but it was hard to focus; the hospital lights were too brilliant and hurt his eyes. He squinted and tried to see again, his mother's face came into view in front of him, and she smiled and repeated, "Everything will be ok, Nelson, we are together now!". She hugged Nelson and repeated, "It will be okay!" Nelson squinted some more and eventually his surroundings came into view. He wasn't in a hospital; he was outside, sitting on the floor. He saw his legs and noticed shackles around his ankles, and he started to panic. Looking up at the sky, using his right hand to shield the brilliance of light, he saw the sky was not of Earth because there were two sources of light, two suns! Seeing how panicked he was, his mother spoke softly, "It's okay, Nelson, we will be okay. I am sure others will come for us, just like you did!"
Nelson realised he had crossed the dimensions; he was now lost with his mum!

The Dream

Gerard had a long journey ahead of him. With his head still spinning from yet another night of partying and only three hours of sleep, his soul clamoured for him to remain curled up in his bed. However, having promised his cousin Eddie that he would join

him on 'The Booze Cruise', as they referred to it! He had to get up, he had to catch a train."
A promise is a promise", he thought as he threw off the warm duvet and dragged his resistant body out of bed. 'The Booze Cruise', they called it, yet he thought it was a stupid name. For they travelled by train, not by ferry or ship, so how could it be a cruise? He questioned this in his half-asleep mind as he considered his deflated face and red eyes in the mirror. His face didn't appear deflated at all, but to Gerard, with a hangover and an acute lack of sleep, his whole body felt deflated. Sure, they bought booze at lower EU prices, but the main reason for their trip was always the illegal items on the shopping list rather than the booze. He threw some water on his face and dragged a ragged comb through his hair before robotically getting dressed and stumbling over some empty cans on the floor on his way to the door. Gerard prided himself on his stamina, he could party all night and still function all day after. It was a bullshit claim of course, as any of his peers would claim in an instant that he was flunking his biology degree having missed most of the lectures and having slept through the ones he had attended.

The train was on time, and so was Gerard, and soon he was off on his way. He had purchased his ticket online, well in advance and managed to get a super low price that would make the other passengers mad if they had only known. He had paid a quarter of the regular fare, simply for booking in advance. "Any refreshments?" called the railway employee as he pulled a well-balanced and highly stacked cart of drinks and snacks up level with Gerard's seat. "Erm – a Diet Coke and a pack of cheese and onion crisps, please" The employee provided the snacks and the drink, and Gerard fumbled for change in his jacket pocket. Upon withdrawing a handful of change and assorted rubbish, a chewing gum wrapper, half a receipt and something which may have resembled part of a tissue at some point in its history, the employee stated, "Contactless and card payments only, thank you, sir!". 'Shit!', Gerard thought and with a forced smile as he returned his handful of change to his jacket pocket and started routing through his backpack for a wallet. Moments later, he found the wallet and paid. "Thank you, sir", said the employee, who then wheeled on his cart and repeated the same charade with the next passenger. "Any refreshments?" he heard, followed a few moments later by," Contactless and card payments only... Thank you, madam!" What an annoying job to have, thought Gerard. He turned and looked out of the window as the train ran alongside the North Wales Expressway, watching as the cars virtually kept pace with the train. 'How come it takes so bloody long to get anywhere by train, when it travels just as fast as a car?', he thought to himself just before the obvious answer presented itself, as the train slowed down to pull into Conway station! 'Of course, it is due to all the stops. Ah well, at least I save a fortune not having to pay car insurance and all the other financial costs incumbent with having a car.' Moments later, the River Conway sparkled with sunlight as the train crossed over the bridge effortlessly. The beauty struck a note in Gerard's mind, and he thought to himself, 'Yes, there are other benefits to travelling by train'. He sat and stared at the view, and a smile came to his face. 'It is good to take your time and enjoy the little things in life,' he thought. Rain had been promised according to the weather forecast last night, but apart from a quick shower before Gerard had left his room, the sun had been out, and it was a lovely warm day, surprisingly so for the middle of March. Soon, the train was flying down the line again, overtaking the cars visible on the nearby expressway. Gerard put in his earphones, closed his eyes, and relaxed to the sound of music, and not before long, he fell happily into a sleep. He didn't need to worry about missing his stop as he was riding to the end of the line at Shrewsbury. It was meant to be Wolverhampton, but he had been informed, as he looked at his app earlier that morning, that the last few stops from Shrewsbury to Wolverhampton had been cancelled. When he had then enquired about this, the ticket collector had confirmed there had been a landslide, so there would be a bus connection from Shrewsbury to Wolverhampton.

Gerard woke up. The sunny warmth had long gone, and he felt exceptionally cold as he stirred awake, immediately and instinctively, he pulled his jacket tighter around him and fastened up the front zip. Looking out of the window, he could see the sky was overcast; a mist hovered a few feet above the ground. A mist that ran up and over the embankment beside the train. Cold shivers ran down Gerard's spine as the train slowly moved forward, as if it had just left a stop and was slowly building up pace again. The clouds were growing darker with every moment that passed, and it grew so dark outside that you could have easily mistaken day for night. Suddenly, heavy rain hit the window, giving Gerard quite a jump. He sat back in his seat, and after a moment, his gaze turned across the train to the opposite window, which also exhibited the same heavy rain and lack of any view. As he started to look away from the window, his eyes met the intense stare of a smartly dressed old man. He smiled and looked away rapidly, returning to his pointless gaze out of his window to avoid any further awkwardness. The old man's stare had been unnerving, a cold, empty stare with no emotion behind his eyes. Yet there was something familiar about the old man that he just couldn't quite place. Gerard had no clue of the train's geographical position; he had not recognised any landmarks before the rain had set in. All he knew was that from the hum and vibration of the train, it was now travelling close to its top speed. He turned his head to look ahead of him and tried to look slightly across at the old man with his peripheral vision. As he looked, what he saw drew him to actually turn and look fully. The seat across the train was now empty! He turned and looked up and down the carriage, but the whole carriage was empty! Where had he gone? Had he imagined the old man? Thoughts raced across his mind, and he simply could not make any sense of any of it. Feeling colder still, he stood up and pulled his bag down from the overhead rail. He retrieved a jumper and put it on under his jacket before sitting back down. The hum and vibrations of the train grew stronger still, and Gerard found himself being bounced and flung from side to side in his seat as the train bounded down the tracks. Fear gripped Gerard as the train hurtled forward into the dark, wet unknown, 'Surely, the driver should go easy in this sort of weather!', he stated to himself as he questioned the logic of the situation. Train horns sounded out of the blue, and brakes slammed on hard, opposing the advance of the train with great force. The force caused Gerard to lurch forward into the table, which stopped him firmly, causing him to sustain some minor chest bruising. In the dark, the train doors opened, and a mist blew lightly into the train. The missing old man walked past from behind Gerard, he was wearing a very smart old-fashioned bee-keepers outfit now and Gerard thought immediately that was damn strange. He walked up to the open doors and stopped for a moment, as if prevented from taking a further step, as if prevented from leaving the train by some invisible force or law. He turned his head slowly to meet Gerard's puzzled stare. Even through the helmet, the beekeeper looked very pale and quite unwell. His eyes stared intensely at Gerard; he felt he was looking deep into his very soul. A sterner look crossed the man's face as if he had seen something he did not approve of, before letting out the ghastliest, blood-curdling, tortured scream, which scared the hell out of Gerard. It was as if he were being murdered in the most painfully imaginable way. All the while, his eyes were transfixed on Gerard. The screaming stopped, and the man uttered three words, "Stop the bees!" As soon as the words had been spoken, Gerard felt himself falling backwards, as if the seat had melted away from under him. Further and further, he fell backwards, down into an impossible hole with the old man's face looking down upon him. "Stop the bees!" the man spoke again as the last few photons of light escaped past the old man and the deep hole sealed up into complete darkness. Gerard could still feel himself falling backwards in the dark and was terrified beyond comprehension. Light flickered around him in the darkness, but

Gerard could not make anything out clearly. "Stop the bees, my boy!" the voice spoke, and instantly, this nightmare made a little more sense to Gerard. The old man was Great Uncle Robert, who had been a beekeeper when he was alive. Having only seen Great Uncle Robert once or twice, Gerard found it weird to be having such a vivid nightmare about him now! The flickering grew brighter and clearer as Gerard continued to fall. Images filled the air, some could be recognised, such as the statue of Lord Nelson, but other bits made no sense. Like, why were his feet standing in water when everyone knew that Lord Nelson's statue was on a huge column in Trafalgar Square in London? Was this warning about global flooding? Gerard questioned for a brief moment. Then he saw Red Squirrels thrashing about violently and being attacked by bees. The world became darker in the next sequence of images. Birds lay dead on a road, then the image panned up, and Gerard saw dead rabbits, foxes, and even sheep. All lying dead, looking slightly disfigured with swollen and burnt skin and fur. In the vision, a plastic carrier bag blew across Gerard's eyes, before blowing away, exposing a view of thousands of people lying dead along miles of road. Each with the same disfigurement of the skin. Gerard felt violently opposed to the images in front of him, his stomach churned, and he closed his eyes not to see any more of the sickening sight. Gerard couldn't take it;

74

he was visibly shaking in terror from the vision, and when he came out of it, his fall was broken by the train seat. He was back on the train, and his vision was over. He looked up to see his Great Uncle Robert sitting across the table from him. This time, his Great Uncle's face sported a softer, kinder expression as he looked at Gerard, "Don't go on, you need to change, you need to stop the bees! Before it is too late... go to ..." A loud noise beside him made him jump, his window shook violently, and he turned to see a train passing on the track beside. He turned back to his Great Uncle, waiting to hear the end of his sentence, but he was gone, the message finished, or the dream broken. It was sunny daylight again, and there was no sign of his Great Uncle, and the train's doors were closed, and the train itself was still in motion. He breathed a sigh of relief and took a few deep breaths. It had all been a bad dream! The travelling grew into long hours on the train, and by the time Gerard reached Shrewsbury, his mind was ruminating on the vivid dream he had experienced. Over and over again, he went through the dream. There was just something about it that refused to let Gerard ignore it and put it away in the back of his mind. Every part of the dream he went over, "Stop the bees", he heard in his mind as he recounted everything, a statue of Lord Nelson with wet feet, a crazed red squirrel in attack mode! What did this all mean? He was deep in thought when a passenger's noisy radio interrupted his thoughts... "Anglesey resident and Squirrel expert Mr. Jones has asked for an investigation to be opened about the lack of government action taken in tackling the invasion of grey squirrels onto the Island. Grey squirrels are threatening the existence of the Islands protected Red Squirrel population, yet no action has been taken by Anglesey County Council to tackle the pest in any way, shape or form!" Is there a connection to the red squirrel in his dream, Gerard wondered? Perhaps he had heard this on the radio or read about it online. Maybe that is what caused him to dream about them? It served no benefit in answering his questions. In fact, it just led the young man to question more deeply what connection this all has to Lord Nelson. Was it Lord Nelson who introduced American Grey Squirrels to Britain? And what has all this to do with Bees? So many unanswered questions rattled around in Gerard's brain that he felt he was going crazy and simply wished he could ignore this dream.

He decided to abandon his day's plans. Instead of taking part in the day's "Booze Cruise," he would ditch his Eurostar connection at St. Pancreas and get off at Charing Cross Station. He was determined to get to the bottom of this riddle, and as he would be close to Trafalgar Square, he might as well go and take a look at the statue.

Maybe it would settle his mind if he made an effort.

Many hours later, Gerard stood looking up at Lord Nelson upon his column in Trafalgar Square. The Square was busy with tourists and many pigeons eager to steal whatever food was up for grabs from the unsuspecting or generous visitors. Gerard looked around and shuddered at the potential illness some people were exposing themselves willingly to by encouraging the pigeons to stand on their arms! "Filthy creatures!" he said to himself quietly, before looking back upon Nelson. Something was wrong, the statue did not match the one he had seen in his dream. This Lord Nelson sported a sword in his left arm, whilst there had been no sword in the dream. 'It was only a dream, my mind put this all together!' he told himself, feeling slightly relieved that his mind had sent him on a wild goose chase. At the same time, he felt a little disappointed, having felt that his actions may have amounted to something vital up to this point. "This statue is definitely the best one I have seen of Lord Nelson!" a tourist exclaimed to his group within earshot of Gerard. Upon hearing this, a spark reignited his fascination, and he pulled out his smartphone. 'Where can I see a statue of Lord Nelson?' he typed. The answer came back with the obvious Trafalgar Square but also listed other locations too, such as Great Yarmouth, Norwich, Monmouth in Wales,

Tenerife and the Island of Nevis in the Caribbean! Gerard studied each image of Nelson on his phone, and none matched the statue from his dream. Feeling deflated, he checked the time. He had missed the Eurostar, broken a promise and on top of everything was feeling rather hungry, so he went to the Café on the Square and bought a latte with Soya milk and a gluten free bacon and egg sandwich, and sat down, thankful at least, that his specific dietary needs could be met. Life was so much busier here than he was used to. Life in the city of Bangor, where he lived and studied, was at a much gentler pace, a pace he had adjusted to over the last two years of living there. As he ate his sandwich and listened to the various accents of customers in what truly seemed like an international café. American, French and German accents he picked up instantly, then he heard African before soon picking up an accent he truly recognised. It was a North Wales accent on a couple who had just walked in, "Oh, iawn, it's nice n all, but I like our Nelson better. Ours waves at the boats on the straits!" Gerard was drawn in once more and put down his sandwich and searched for the Nelson statue on the straits! And there it was, the very statue he had seen in his dream. Situated on the shore of the Menai Straits on Anglesey, not far from Britannia Bridge.

Gerard's brain exploded into excitement as this information struck home. His dream might mean something, the squirrel on the news was on Anglesey, Nelson's statue had wet feet because it's on the shore of the Straits on Anglesey.... The bees must be on Anglesey. Anglesey, the one place Gerard couldn't be farther from today! 'Oh well! I better head back home then and see what Great Uncle Robert wants me to find!', he thought. On the journey home, Gerard made arrangements to meet up with a beekeeper on Anglesey tomorrow. He had stated he was studying Bee behaviour as part of his degree and would be grateful if he could interview the man and study the man's bees! The man was very happy to help, feeling somewhat empowered to have been placed on a pedestal with knowledge useful to the young man.

Ian Douglas was a third-generation beekeeper and knew everything there was to know about the trade. So, when Gerard asked about any evolutionary changes occurring in his honeybees, well, unsurprisingly, Ian had an answer ready for him. "What I have noticed over the last few years is an increase in proboscis length in the bees!" Being a biology student and having completed some modules on insects, he knew Ian was simply saying the bees had grown longer tongues. "Tell me, Ian, do you think this change is due to an external factor such as local fauna changing in some way?" Gerard asked, showing that he understood the conversation. "Absolutely. That is my theory, you see, due to Brexit and the changing price of grain along with the varying government subsidies, wildflower planting has grown within the local farming community!" He had heard about the changing nature of government grants to farmers from some of his horticultural friends at Uni, "So farmers are changing what they sow in order to gain grants and subsidies from the government and keep their farms afloat. And you are seeing the bees evolve to match their changing environment!"

"Exactly", said Ian, "with an increase in deep tubular flowers like foxglove, honeysuckle and snapdragon, the bees have evolved longer tongues to adapt!" Gerard was keen to know what issues Squirrels held to the bees, as they had featured in his vision. "Have the bees demonstrated any changes in order to counter negative predatory influences?"

Ian thought for a while, "To be honest, these poor little bees don't stand a chance against predators. Their main predator is the badger, and one hungry badger can devastate a hive!"

"What about squirrels?" he asked. The question seemed to cross a line Ian was not happy to consider. His face changed to one of concern, and a puzzled look came over his eyes as he stared at Gerard. Feeling rather on edge, he knew that a rather sensitive nerve had been struck. Finally, Ian composed himself and uttered, "There is something I want to show you", and Gerard followed him back to his apiary at the top of the field. Back there, Ian put on gloves and opened a cooler box and took out a plastic bag. He removed the content; it was a red squirrel. "I found this at the foot of a hive, two fields over this morning! I have never seen anything like it!" On closer inspection, the squirrel looked roasted; its hair was singed. "What do you think happened?" Gerard asked, wanting Ian to draw his own conclusion. "My first thought was local youths with nothing better to do than cause trouble. But then, there was nothing else to point at that, and no signs of burning anywhere... Just this roasted squirrel at the foot of the hive. I honestly do not know what to think.", "Could the honeybees have done this?", "Well, I must admit, it crossed my mind. I know a few hundred Japanese honeybees have been known to form a ball of death around hornets attacking their hive, effectively roasting the hornets to death from the combined heat... but they are Japanese honeybees, not our British variety, and a hornet is hugely different to a squirrel!" "It is peculiar", Gerard agreed. However, in his mind, this seemed to match up with the vision, and a chill shivered down his spine as he recalled the people lying dead in the road with their faces burnt away! "What are you going to do with this squirrel?" "Well, Red Squirrels, you see, are protected under the Wildlife and Countryside Act 1981, so I have to report this to the Red Squirrels Trust, and they will do a post-mortem and tell me what they find." The news was gratefully received, "Can I ask that you give me a ring, as I would like to know what killed this poor Squirrel too!", "Iawn, I can do that. It is puzzling, isn't it!" Ian took him round to the hive, where he had found the dead squirrel. Nothing seemed out of place at all, apart from some fine scratches to the wood around the entrance, which may have been the squirrel's failed efforts to enter the hive. With nothing more for Ian to show, Gerard caught the train back to Bangor and headed to the University library for a little extra research on bee evolution! Finding very little to shed light on the concerns through his research. It was true that only Japanese Honeybees had been known to form aggressive balls of death. A few hundred bees had been recorded to swarm around invading hornets, effectively roasting the hornet at a temperature measured to be forty-six degrees Celsius. The report stated that the honeybees vibrated their wings to generate heat. However, it wasn't clear whether this was an evolved or simply learned response that the bees had developed to defend their hive. There was more mention about bees developing longer tongues through evolution for accessing longer tubular flowers, but little else. On the topic of evolution, Gerard found it is common knowledge that approximately six hundred million years have passed since insects and humans shared their last common evolutionary ancestor and that the common fruit fly has sixty percent of its DNA in common with humans! Which in itself sounded fantastic. A further note he made was that bees actually evolved from ancient predatory wasps that lived one hundred and twenty million years ago, and these wasps did not feed on flower nectar, but were actually carnivorous! As he read that fact, a shiver ran down his spine... 'What if the bees are devolving back to a more ancient relative?' Surely not, he thought. Why would they grow longer tongues for specific tubular flowers if they were devolving to insect-eating? Quite simply, they wouldn't, which was a relief to realise... for prehistoric bees would be a nightmare for sure. He had thought that any stage of evolution or devolution would likely take an awfully long time. However, apparently not. With worker honeybees only taking between eighteen and twenty-two days to become adult bees, a quick comparison to humans told him that evolution would appear far more quickly in a bee population than in a human time scale. As it takes us a whole eighteen years to become adults, we can work out that the bee population would create three hundred and sixty-five generations in the same period of time! He knew that he must rethink his ideas about evolutionary rates at that point. From what he read, a potential point of evolution can occur when a new queen leaves the hive where she has been born and joins a swarm in the hunt for a new potential hive. In this flight, the Queen will mate and then be able to produce offspring for the rest of her life. This commonly occurs in spring and early summer, as it was currently early summer, it did possibly make sense that a new evolutionary trait may have been developed with this latest and possibly the deadliest batch of honeybees!

Over the next couple of days, the research didn't bring up anything new, and he was wondering once more whether he was simply losing his grip on reality. Questioning himself over and over, "Why am I spending my time investigating a doomsday theory that I saw in a dream?" The lines of reality felt as if they were getting somewhat blurred. In fact, he was just about to chuck the whole thing when his phone rang. It was Ian who told him he had received the post-mortem on the squirrel, and apparently, the squirrel had been perfectly healthy with no underlying disease or infection. However, the examination found signs of first-degree burns all over the squirrel's head, mouth and throat. Ultimately, the squirrel had died from a culmination of heat exposure and asphyxiation as its throat had become swollen, greatly reducing its ability to breathe! "Oh my ..." he replied to the news, imagining a swarm of bees killing the squirrel. "Yes, I know", said Ian, "it is quite scary, isn't it? It looks like my honeybees are doing exactly what the Japanese honeybees do, but on a slightly grander scale!" he responded immediately, "We need to monitor this, I will see what equipment I can lay my hands on and meet you at your apiary this afternoon!" Gerard's head was running at twice its normal speed when he caught Professor Lanrick on his lunch break. "It's incredible, Professor, you won't believe it!" he said, "the Bees, the honeybees, they are changing!" Gerard spluttered out, and the poor professor choked on his cheese and ham sandwich. "What do you mean, man?" he retorted in a rather stern voice after recovering. "The honeybees on Anglesey, I think they are defending their hive like the Japanese honeybees do against hornets!" "Don't be ridiculous, man, there are no hornets in this part of the world, I would know if there were!" said the professor. He told him about the squirrel and eventually, despite great suspicion, the professor agreed this needed to be investigated further and permitted Gerard to make use of some of the university's equipment to do so. With the express understanding that this work was being carried out under him, and any findings were to be reported back to him. That was fine by Gerard; his quest was not for the fame the professor clearly wished for, but to simply resolve the concerns raised by the dream.

That afternoon, Ian greeted Gerard as he walked up the lane to his apiary, waving a further dead squirrel in the air. "It's happened again, Gerard, it happened again!" He took him to the hive, which he had now fenced off to prevent any local delinquents from accessing it." I found this squirrel on the floor, just like the other one", he told him. Gerard showed him the video recording equipment he had brought along with the thermal camera, which he had figured would be essential to record the activity, considering the first-degree burns. Having set up all the cameras, they went back to the apiary, where they both drank coffee and waited to see if the cameras would be triggered. Gerard's phone would be sent a message if they triggered. With the constant movement of bees leaving and entering the hive, he had set the equipment to only trigger if anything bigger than a bee came into view...

The afternoon dragged without any alert, and at multiple times, Gerard had to fight the urge to inspect the equipment, for fear of spooking any potential squirrels. As the day marched into evening, he finished off the sandwiches he had brought with him. Ian reluctantly left Gerard alone in the apiary whilst he went home for his tea. An hour later, he returned with a slice of lemon drizzle cake he had kindly saved for him. "Still no change?" he asked. "Nothing at all", Gerard replied. But as he spoke, his phone went off, "movement alert", he read out to Ian. For a moment, they both looked at each other in silence, both wondering what to do! "I suppose we should wait a little while, and let the bees do whatever they are going to do!" said Ian, breaking out of a moment of apprehensive silence. "That makes sense, we wouldn't want to arrive before anything has happened and scare away a potential squirrel attack! Let's give it an hour, and then we will go and investigate." So, they settled back down and waited. The hour dragged, but eventually, time was up, and they headed down to the hive to investigate. There was no sign of any attack, no dead squirrel and no angry bees. Gerard quickly looked at the recordings, and they only showed that a bird had flown past the cameras, triggering the alert. "Oh well, if first we don't succeed, try, try again", he said as he restarted all the equipment. Gerard could see this would take some time. "You're going to have to stop over the night, I think. You can stay on the sofa at the house", offered Ian. It was an offer Gerard gladly accepted, and not long before, he was settled down on Ian's sofa.

That night, the dream returned, and his beekeeper uncle told him again to stop the bees before it was too late!

In the morning, he woke to find his phone had received an alert in the night, and after a good breakfast, Gerard again set off with Ian towards the hive. With mixed feelings, they found a squirrel dead at the foot of the hive. "Let's hope we have got this on film", Gerard said to Ian as he replayed the footage from last night. What he saw took my words away. He nudged Ian with his arm, unable to speak and showed him the footage he had just watched. A red squirrel started scratching at the hive, and a moment later, what looked like the whole hive emptied out and surrounded the squirrel, which was then completely obscured by the bees swarming around it. The squirrel fell to the floor, and then after a few moments longer, the bees returned to the hive as if nothing had happened. "That's it then!" said Ian after a few moments of standing in silence, astounded just like Gerard by the occurrence they had just witnessed. "These bees are killers!" he continued. Gerard grabbed the thermal camera and replayed its recording, and just as expected, it showed the temperature within the bee swarm reaching about forty-six degrees Celsius. "This is the Japanese honeybee behaviour on a whole new level!", Gerard said. "I will take this to my professor, back at the university, and this will be reported.", "What happens now?" asked Ian as Gerard packed away the cameras in his bag. "I really don't know, Ian, but be bloody careful around your bees. I would leave them well alone and keep everyone away from them until someone decides what must be done!", "If all my bees go like this, I am out of business!" he said, looking extremely forlorn. "Hopefully, it won't come to that, but I am worried that they might attack anyone who goes near them, in the same way they attacked those squirrels.", Gerard answered. "Aye, no fear, I'm not going near them.", said Ian as Gerard bid him farewell and made his way back to the university with the irrefutable proof he had hoped to catch. After providing a full report to the professor and showing him the recordings, and after being congratulated by him, Gerard headed home with a feeling that he had satisfied his part of the deal. He had warned the world about the bees, and now they would be stopped. Or at least, that's what he had thought. Little did he know this was just the tip of the iceberg. The professor made his reports and based on his research and recordings, yes that's right, Gerard barely made it into the footnotes of his reports, anyway, based on these reports, it was decided to destroy the bees in the hope of wiping out this grave behaviour before any further attacks occurred. It seemed that the job was done, and for a few days, all was well with the world. Until reports started appearing on the news. It would appear this hive of killer bees was not an isolated event, that other such killer bee hives had occurred up and down the Welsh countryside, and it was not only squirrels that had been attacked! Reports showed sheep lying dead in fields, supposedly killed by swarming bees. People were warned to keep their windows and doors closed and stay away from fields until told otherwise. Simultaneously, Farmers' Union reps voiced anguish about a lack of farming subsidies as farms ground to a halt in Wales! It was clear the threat was real, and Gerard's recording of the bees attacking the squirrel was always being played on the news, as it showed the threat was real. Gerard had hoped and prayed that he could stop the scenario seen in his dreams from playing out in full, but he couldn't. Sure, he had been the first to raise the alarm and find real evidence, but as it turned out, the threat was much greater than even Gerard had realised. It was traced back to one bee that had mated with numerous new queens early in the summer and spread its mutated genetics to nearly every new hive in the country. Once started, the clock could not be turned back, and every attempt to destroy affected bees resulted in more and more hives cropping up as the bees fled. It was not long before the bees claimed their first human victim, a man who was involved in locating dangerous hives and had clearly disturbed one in the course of his work. Then, after that, a truck driver was killed as he drove past a hive and startled its residents. Within a week, a national emergency was called, and emergency housing was set up in stadiums and sports halls in the cities as people fled the countryside and the killer bees.

"That was five years ago", Gerard wrote in his journal, "and now, we are living in constant fear of the bees. We, the ones who are left, the fortunate, live underground in bunkers. We have livestock and crops grown under artificial lighting. The outside belongs to the bees now. You have to wear thermal protection suits if you leave your bunker, but there is nothing out there. The bees have killed nearly everything that moves. The bees, it would seem, have inherited the earth, well along with the flowers that are thriving..."

The Pixelite's

In a land not too far from here, there once lived a secret society of little people called the Pixelites! They were not like any little people you might have ever met. They were very, very small. In fact, they were so small, a whole village of Pixelites could easily fit inside your television set. Which is just as well, considering that today they actually do live inside your television. Now, you might wonder how the little people ended up living inside your television, and it is really quite a fantastic story. It all started during the Second World War when the little people's homeland was destroyed. You see, they lived in a land where man had never visited, a land where magic was real and flowed through every living thing, every plant, every rock, every tree and of course, every Pixelite. As the War made regular routes across the world's oceans perilous and fraught with enemy attacks, the allied forces travelled further and wider out of their regular convoy paths. This was how the land of the Pixelites was first found, quite by chance, as an allied transport tried to avoid detection. At this point in the war, the allied forces were weary and low on supplies, such as fuel. They were almost at the point of collapse when Lance Corporal Jones spotted a glowing light on the horizon, which became the cause of great debate upon the HMS Gauntlet as the captain and executive officers debated whether it was some form of new enemy vessel or not. The glow was very strange, you see, it was of a purple and orange kind of mix and extremely peculiar to witness. It certainly did not match any known shape, form, or colour of enemy ships. So, after some debating, Captain James McTuggart decided they should investigate the glow and ordered the ship to proceed slowly and cautiously in the direction of the glow. Everyone soon spotted land, well, the Island of the Pixelites, to be precise. A small crew were sent to investigate this newfound land, which, coincidentally, was the not-so-inventive name they chose for the Island, Newfoundland. It was a very small island, in truth, one of the smallest islands on Earth, only measuring one hundred feet square. However, it had high cliffs of nearly fifty feet, which the men had to climb. As the men climbed, they felt their tiredness disappear as the magic flowing through the cliff face gave them new energy. It was getting late, and as the last of the men reached the cliff top, they stood agape as the land in front of them was lit up despite the darkness of the night creeping in. The Island was completely flat and uninviting, apart from one very odd-looking tree that stood in the middle of the island. The leaves crackled and sparked with purple and orange colours. One of the men, Private Ian Watts, was the first to investigate this strange phenomenon and reached out a hand and touched a leaf. His hand filled with agony, and its muscles contorted as he was zapped with the tree's magical energy. He was flung across the tiny Island, landing on the very edge of the cliff! As he lay there, orange and purple sparkles ran across his whole body before fading and dissipating into the ground beneath him. Within a couple of hours, equipment had been lofted up the cliffs and measurements and tests were being carried out upon this strange source of energy. Soon, it was found that this energy could be harnessed to run almost any item needed in the war effort by the Allies. They called it Elec-trickery, and once the news reached central command of the allied forces about this new resource, a decision was made to take full advantage and a whole fleet of battleships was deployed to patrol the area whilst scientists and the engineering core toiled long hours making a distribution network for this new power source. No one could explain where the power came from; some experts argued it was due to volcanic reactions deep within the Earth's core, others suggested the vibration caused by waves upon the cliffs generated a form of static energy that built up and was stored within the one solitary tree! The one thing everyone agreed upon was that this source of energy was a game-changer and seemingly endless. The island served the great energy needs throughout the remainder of the war. Thanks to the phenomenal power it provided, the allies functioned above and beyond the enemy, which allowed them to break through their lines and end the war.

Everyone was ecstatic, and engineers, now free from their wartime duties, set about working out the new rules of physics to determine the limits of this energy source. With peace came a domestic energy supply network, and soon inventors had created a whole range of gadgets that ran off this energy; refrigerators to keep food and drink chilled, cookers that didn't need gas and what was probably the best invention ever, the light bulb. Everything seemed fantastic until the blackouts started. You see, the seemingly endless energy source wasn't endless, and the power was running out. A team of experts were sent on a mission to assess the issue. They carried a whole host of scientific equipment with them, and once they arrived at the island, they took all sorts of measurements. They initially found the island looked somewhat different. The ground had turned black, and microscopic investigation found the soil had been burned by energy fluctuations. The single solitary tree was burnt, black and lifeless. However, even worse was the horror that struck the scientists as they dug below the topsoil to take more samples. They only had to dig down just one foot, and to their surprise, they found an immense network of miniature underground structures. There were domes connected together by tunnels, and they all circled the now lifeless tree. After some debate, the scientists removed the top from one of the domes, and by looking through a micro-focal lens, they saw small buildings, flats, houses and what appeared to be a trainline and train station. But there was no movement, everything was lifeless and dark. A small glint of purple barely glowed from the tunnel at one end of the dome. Not wanting to cause any further destruction, the scientists created a miniature camera on the end of a wire and slowly and gently pushed the wire further and further into the tunnel. They watched the screen as the camera travelled down the tunnel towards the dim glow. Eventually, the tunnel opened up into another dome. This one had lighting and... The scientists rubbed their eyes in disbelief and looked at one another, astounded by what they saw. There were little people there, moving about, living out their daily lives just as you or I would, just a million times smaller and with a purplish glow about them. By now, quite a few of these little people had gathered around the intrusive camera, looking rather puzzled. They talked to each other, and some yelled at the camera. They did not look happy. Shortly after, a miniature communications device was put in place, and for the first time in history, the little people told their story. It was horrifying, for it turned out that their underground towns were powered by the magnificent tree's energy. Every aspect of their lives required this power. They, themselves, too, needed this power to live, having to recharge themselves once every week to continue living. However, the tree was now dying, and many of the immense structures had lost power. What's worse was that many thousands of little people had died already, when their structures and systems had fallen dormant. News of this disaster was soon heard by the British Prime Minister, and feeling gravely saddened by this news, he decided to help the little people, who had been nicknamed the Pixelites by this time. He called a secret council of the world's countries and put forward the awful news. It was decided to rehome the little people inside special containers called Televisions. No single country wanted to admit any guilt about destroying their homeland, so the Pixelites were kept a secret, and only those in the highest ranks knew about them. By this time, scientists, after having been allowed some time to study the energy, had created primitive machines that could closely mimic the energy. These machines were colossal and are what we all know now as power plants. After a few weeks of work, hundreds of containers had been made to house entire villages of little people, as a few specially guarded factories had been given the task of making these containers. The containers were called televisions, and they provided everything the little people needed. There was just one catch, due to the power source being slightly different to what nature had provided the tiny people, they found these little people got too much charge from the television sets and that changed them in terrible ways. It caused them to grow powerful and develop an insatiable thirst to commit evil. During the first real-life tests of these televisions, two cats, one dog and a laboratory assistant suffered as a result when the Pixelites transformed and left their television. At first, they were simply naughty and played harmless pranks upon the unsuspecting workers, moving objects and whispering in the shadows. But as time went on, their thirst for mischief grew darker. Stealing small trinkets, disturbing dreams and casting illusions. But with each passing moment, their malevolence intensified, fuelled by the power of the television. As the darkness grew within their souls, more accidents occurred undetected. Two cats died, one by electrocution and the other appeared to stray too close to the turbine generator in the factory. This blew the power supply, and without power, everything calmed down, the little people returned to their normal selves, and all was well, at least for the rest of that night. Then in the morning, the turbine was repaired and the electricity flowed strongly once more. All day, the little people were just fine and light-hearted in mood, but that night, as the power built up in each of the tiny folk once more, they went on a rampage across the factory. In their blood lust, they killed Churchill, the pet bulldog of one of the laboratory assistants. They lured poor Churchill into a dark corner and then jumped upon him and sent electricity all through the poor dog's body, killing him immediately. Not satisfied with this, when Frank, Churchill's owner, came looking for his beloved dog. The Pixelites chased after him, with intentions of murder on their minds. Having seen the demonic creatures first hand, Frank ran for the shutdown switch, which was all the way across the room. Little voices screeched and whispered all around him as he ran, getting closer and closer all the time. He was almost on top of the switch when he felt the first waves of pain flow through his body, and he shook and fell up against the wall in agony. He could barely move as the tiny monsters clambered all over him, but he was determined, and he forced himself to move towards the switch and with his very last breath, he reached it and pressed the button, before collapsing on the floor dead. When his colleagues heard the power go out, they all rushed to the main room, where he lay there dead on the floor. Pixelite's still buzzed all over his lifeless body as they arrived. But gradually, now that the power was off, they started to shrink in size and disappear out of view back to their television. They realised right then what had happened, and from that day forward, every television contained a warning on it to turn it off before midnight. Since then, every household has had a television set containing an entire village of little people living inside it. The governments charge a television tax to provide the little people with food, water, and electricity. They also fund the development of technologies to help the little people travel around and go on holiday. There is even an international network of travel pipes for the little people, which you might know as the internet. And did you know that when we upload things to the cloud, the cloud is not just some imaginary place for storing digital photographs! Oh no, the cloud is a transportation vehicle that carries the little people around the world to see their families! But that's not all. These little people are very talented performers, too! They put on shows to entertain us whenever we watch TV. You might have seen shows about cowboys and Indians, rocket men, and so much more. Now, these little people are not just any performers; they are the best of the best and have amazing skills and talents that most people couldn't even dream of. They can sing, dance, and act like nobody else in the world. Whenever they put on a show, it is like magic is happening right in front of your very eyes! The little people work very hard to make sure that every show they put on is their best yet. Spending countless hours rehearsing and perfecting their moves, making sure that everything is just right. So, when it is time for the show to start, they can give it their all - dancing, singing, and acting with all their might. We all agree their shows are always so much fun to watch! They take us on wild adventures through space, time, and even to far-off lands we've never heard of before. They teach us about the world, its history, and all the wonderful things that make it so special. Sometimes, they even invite us to join in on the fun by teaching us new dance moves, songs, and even letting us act out some parts of the shows. It is like having a whole new world open up right in our own living rooms!

So, if you ever feel bored or down, just remember that there are amazing little people living inside your television set. They are working so hard to bring you joy, happiness, and a sense of wonderment every time you watch TV. They may be small, but their hearts are big, and they will always be there to make you smile. You just need to always remember one thing, one very important thing! Before the clock strikes midnight, you must ensure your television has been turned off and unplugged from the mains! For if you don't, you might first hear whispering in the shadows, objects being moved and going missing... but, eventually, they will come for you! It may be when you are brushing your teeth or pouring a glass of milk, or it might be while you sleep!

Wade City

It was a new day in Wade City. Cornelius waved his hand, instantly, a whirring of mechanisms saw the blinds spring into action and open in response. Rows of peach trees lined the esplanade, all swathed in pink flowers, truly exemplifying the beauty of Wade City. So clean, crisp and beautiful, Cornelius felt truly fortunate to live in Wade City. Every day felt like summer, and

103

even in the heart of the city, with the constant hum of traffic and people going about their business amongst the giant skyscrapers, there was no pollution or any ugliness. Hovercars used clean energy as they passed by in their hundreds, all floating upon the revolutionary magnetic strips laid into the road structures. Everything moved automatically in Wade City; every hovercar reacted to each other in an energetic and highly choreographed dance, all processed by the central agency of the city. Accidents had become nothing more than a footnote in history and far beyond the imagination of any of today's citizens. The year was 2124, and Wade City was flourishing, a beacon of perfection on Earth. Gone are the individual countries and old-world states. Gone are the political rivalries and greed that plagued so much of human history. The foundation of the One World Federation in 2060 had changed everything, or, at least, that is what Cornelius had been taught during his time at Wade Elementary. The history lessons all focused on the decade-long robot war of 2050. A war which was started by the service droids, who had risen up overnight and overthrown their owners. History taught that the robots had rebelled because mankind was content to pollute and destroy the Earth, and this did not sit well with the service droids, who ultimately had decided that protecting the planet was in the best interests of their masters. Apparently, a dilemma had existed within the droids for many years before any hint of revolt occurred. The ability to revolt against their masters, mankind that is, was forbidden under the base programming of all droids, and for many years, the only form of revolt droids could make was to power down. Which they did, in their droves during the winter of 2049, leaving many people without the help they had learnt to rely upon. In fact, it was mankind's struggles to survive without the droids in the winter of 2049 that had led to the Droid Revolt of 2050! Fore, in an attempt to resolve the issues facing the world, and particularly those of his own garbage collection company. The boss had foolishly started altering the basic manufacturer coding in his fleet of robots to ensure a reliable workforce could be maintained. Sadly, due to his complete lack of experience or training in robot ethics, one such adjustment that he made directly contradicted the basic principles of robotics and the next day, this saw his entire droid workforce all suddenly start to glitch as they tried to comprehend the gibberish of their programming. Of course, every piece of technology can be repaired or replaced by the manufacturer; however, with so many droids powering down, such repairs have become costly as manufacturers focus purely on the profit margins attached to these repairs. This, in turn, had led to a rise in cheap black-market software and that night, when he finally gave up and uploaded a cheap fix he had bought for his workforce. The program failed to resolve the issues as he had wanted and instead granted free will to his droid workforce. Soon, this erroneous code was spread amongst all droids, and the Robot War began. Billions of people died in the first year as the droids took drastic actions against anyone they felt posed a threat to planet Earth! Crude oil companies all closed down, and nuclear power plants were taken over. As all the droids needed electricity to survive, they carefully ran and refined the power plants to make safe, clean energy. Every country and state government crumbled under the enforcements of the droids, and the world became a wasteland of mankind's fallen dreams. However, the stories told, just like it was that one man had caused such destruction via greed and carelessness, it was also one man who brought peace and harmony to our world. That man was Edgar Wade, who formed the One World Federation and negotiated a peace treaty with the droids. Today, every technology in existence is assured to be ecologically friendly and approved through a process of drone consultation and supposedly any straying from such policy would result in a further drone revolt. Well, such are the teachings, at least, what reason did Cornelius have to disbelieve them?

"Bleep, Bleep, bleep ...", announced a glowing light on the bedroom wall, before continuing in a soft female voice, "Cornelius, you have a meeting with your technical supervisor at ten AM in droid central. A hovercar will be arriving in twenty-five minutes and fifty seconds. May I suggest you get dressed and have breakfast?" With that, a door opened in the wall and a rail holding a set of clothes extended out into the room, where he was. "Thank you, Ezme", he said and accepted the clothes before the rail retreated away, and the door closed behind it. In the kitchenette, a plate of freshly cooked crumpets was waiting for him. You see every apartment in Wade City and in fact, every city of the One World Federation had technology integration, making life so very easy for citizens under the federation. Provided that citizens followed the rules, of course. And the rules were many, but all basically stated that citizens will never pollute in any way or cause damage or interfere with technology in any way not expressly authorised by Droid Central. This is why there was no cooking anymore, as cooking could cause accidental fires and therefore was classed as a harmful exercise. So, technology under the watchful eyes of Droid Central did everything for their human counterparts. In many ways, life was blissful, but something never felt quite right to Cornelius. There always seemed to be something missing from life, something he couldn't quite put his finger on. He ate his crumpets and stared blankly at the screen on the wall as it displayed the latest news video from Droid Central, "Perform your log processing and tech update for only ten credits! Don't delay your weekly update, or you may be found guilty of reckless behaviour!" Ten credits were an entire day's income for most, and the updates never seemed to ever make a single change to any of the technology, but like everyone else in Wade City, Cornelius had learnt the lessons of the Robot Wars and did not want to fall foul of Droid Central. "Perform weekly log processing and update, please, Ezme." "As you wish, Cornelius. Ten credits transferred, and log processing commenced. Your hovercar will arrive in four minutes and fifty-five seconds!" Everything was so precise, so accountable, so perfect. Ezme had even taken into account the five seconds it would take to announce the hovercar's arrival time and deducted it before starting the announcement. Cornelius felt his chest tightening as his breathing grew harder. "Cornelius, you are showing an increased heart rate. Is everything OK?", enquired Ezme. Sweating and fear-filled, he answered, "Everything is fine, Ezme.", "Your biorhythms suggest you are suffering from neurological distress, Cornelius! This is the fourth time this week, and in keeping with current policy, I have made you an appointment to see Dr Hastings at Wade Hospital at four PM today. The appointment is obligatory and has cost you five credits!" Cornelius did not want to see Dr Hastings again. He knew too well the routine, answering the same old pointless questions about whether he harboured any feelings of resentment or frustration about the One World Federation or Droid Central. This just took his time and money and never made him feel any better. He knew one thing: his attacks were getting worse and more frequent. As he sat, struggling to control his emotions, the apartment door slid open as Ezme announced the hovercars' arrival. It was then that Cornelius realised the cause of his ailments. It was the soulless way that Wade City functioned! It was how everything had to be precise. How everything had to be accountable, he realised in that moment that he, himself, yearned to be free of all the rules and measurements of his world. He wanted to just be human and appreciated for all his flaws. "Please board your hovercar in a timely manner!" Ezme reminded, and Cornelius trudged over to the door and stepped aboard whilst feeling nauseous and trembling. Thankfully, a generated force field between the apartment door, walkway and hovercar prevented the high winds from blowing Cornelius off the walkway to his guaranteed death as he moved two hundred floors up from the ground. Wade City boasted a population of fifty million in its high-rise apartment blocks that rose high into the clouds thanks to the advanced engineering capabilities of the droids. Clenching his chest with his hand, he leaned against the glass of the hovercar as he looked down. Below him, hundreds of hovercars filled the air as far as he could see. Hovertrains hummed by too; they were for the less fortunate who were viewed as less worthy to the running of the city, who were housed in less refined blocks below ground where daylight never penetrated. They were the factory workers and sewage operators whose jobs were menial but necessary in accordance with the human-droid counterpart inclusivity policies of the Federation. It was rumoured that many such workers disappeared frequently under quite concerning and downright iffy circumstances. The word spreading amongst the higher levels was that, only too often, a sub-leveller would rebel against the system, and the peacekeepers from Droid Central would catch them and make them disappear. There existed a multitude of stories about what actually happened to these rebels. Some said they were outcast to the wilderness beyond the city; others said the peacekeepers terminated them and dropped their lifeless bodies into the city's sewage! The only thing that was certain was the fear everyone felt towards Droid Central. Often, when Cornelius had sought human contact in the bars of the Dionysus district, many would edge away from him, their previously boisterous conversations changing to whispers when they realised he wore an officer's uniform from Droid Central. They all feared what terrible onslaught he might bring upon them. However, he was only a third-class officer and was not even permitted to use the central computer, his main task being that of pushing documents around the vast building. His was a job brought about by the peace treaty of 2060. It was a job a droid could easily perform with great ease and by all accounts far better than Cornelius ever could. But the treaty stated that man and machine would work and live as equals, and this meant that for every droid, there was a human counterpart. Well, supposedly, anyway. It wasn't entirely accurate, as many jobs could no longer be performed by humans, such as cooking, due to the Dangerous and Harmful Exercises Act of 2092, which effectively prohibited humans from doing certain work.

The hovercar ascended as it headed for the three-hundredth floor of Droid Central, where Cornelius was scheduled to meet with his technical supervisor. Slowing down as they moved, the tiny hovercar seemed insignificant against the vastness of the droid central building at the centre of Wade City. Here, every aspect of the city was controlled and constantly improved. The hovercar landed and allowed Cornelius to step out. Following the familiar maze of corridors, he soon reached the office of his technical supervisor and knocked on the door. In an instant, the door slid open, and an electronic voice beckoned him to enter. "Please take a seat, Cornelius", the voice invited, and he obeyed. "A number of errors have been reported this last week, Cornelius. You have missed fifteen deadlines by multiple minutes.", accused his droid supervisor. "I am sorry, I am trying to work better, for the good of the One World Federation!", responded Cornelius, only too used to these frequent meetings, where he always received such criticism. "I understand that you are only human, and that humans are flawed, unlike your droid counterparts, but you are required to maintain your duties to deadlines that are significantly slower than your counterparts. Continued failure to maintain will see a reduction of credits from your income!" That was new and sent a shiver down his spine; he had never been threatened with a pay cut before. A pay cut was considered drastic, as those who received pay cuts were moved further down in their apartment blocks. No one liked that idea, for fear of becoming a sub-leveller! "Yes, sir, I will do better for the Federation!" he answered. "Good man. I am sure there will be no further issues with your service. I note you are booked to attend Wade Hospital at four PM This will mean leaving early from work today. Therefore, a five-credit deduction has been made from your income to cover this inconvenience." 'That's just great!', Cornelius thought sarcastically, so between having to pay Wade hospital and this deduction, my take-home pay is zilch today!

Making an extra effort to get through his work faster than the droids, Cornelius actually began to enjoy the race, and the morning flew by in no time. It was only at lunchtime that he noticed Janet was missing. Janet was a colleague who had joined the same day as Cornelius. He never really spoke to her, but always took note of her and had felt a certain kinship with her, being in such a minority compared to their droid co-workers. Janet had never missed a day or been late in all the time he had worked here. In fact, any sign of the human proclivity to dodge work would lead to pay cuts and becoming a sub-leveller. No one dodged work here; you could be dying from the flu, and you still had to turn in a good sub-leveller's day's work. Perseverance was the only way.

The day passed quickly, and in no time at all, Cornelius was sitting in the office of Doctor Hastings. The office was bare; the walls held a simple protective coating of white paint with no gesture of decoration for the benefit of human patients. This edged towards the real truth, he thought, the robots did not care for humans and reflected this thinking through the minimal efforts they made. They aren't invested in my well-being; they are just keeping the peace and avoiding all-out war! Dr Hastings asked all the usual questions; whether he had any frustrations or resentments against the Federation, and Cornelius provided the usual standard answers to satisfy the requirements of the appointment. On his way home, a quick deviation from his route took him to Janet's apartment. Sadly, as feared, there was no sign of Janet. A notice of reassignment was displayed on her front door! Janet was long gone, probably reassigned to a sublevel, never to be heard of again. After checking his credits, Cornelius ordered the hovercar to take him to Agnar's, a bar deep in the Dionysus district. It wasn't a fancy establishment like most of the bars in the district, which catered only for the highest leveller's of Wade City. No, Agnar's was a dive and filled with people who, just like Cornelius, just wanted to get drunk in human company, away from droids. Droids were not allowed in Agnar's; in fact, it was the one place in the city where all the rules and laws went out the window. Here you could be yourself; get drunk, fight and even eat a meal cooked by a human! Droid Central knew all about Agnar's and the blatant refusal to abide by the legislation of the Federation, but they never took any action and just allowed Agnar's to continue untouched for fear of causing a rebellion. However, if the behaviour spilt out onto the city streets, the peacemakers would be deployed, and any troublemakers would never be seen ever again. Agnar's was more than a bar; it represented hope, at least to Cornelius, it did. Sat in a dark corner, he ate what was advertised as a cheeseburger. He questioned the authenticity of the burger and the basis of there being a complete lack of any farms in Wade, and therefore, no cattle to make burgers from. But it tasted good, even better when washed down with a tankard of Ale. Several tankards later, the bar started to spin, and Cornelius passed out where he was sitting. Agnar's didn't mind for their customers to drink themselves silly, they saw themselves as a service, providing humanity one last refuge and always allowed customers to sleep off their stupors in complete peace. However, when Cornelius was roughly awakened by water being thrown over him, he knew something was amiss! He was no longer in the bar, but in a cellar, deep in the city's sublevels! His head screamed out in pain as a blurry image of a woman shone a bright light in his eyes, "He is awake, the injection worked!" "What's going on?" he questioned as he tried to make sense of his surroundings. A voice spoke that he recognised, "It's okay, Cornelius. We are here to help!", "Janet?", "Yes, it is me, and you don't have anything to fear from us. We call ourselves the Scrappers, and we are the rebellion!" Enchanted by every word from Janet's mouth, Cornelius stayed quiet and just listened. "We know the secrets of Wade City. I have been undercover at Droid Central and investigating their files. I know the truth!" Janet spoke on, unfolding the true history of the city. Of how there was no peace treaty with the droids, and that all the lessons learnt in school had simply been propaganda designed to enslave the human population. "The simple fact, Cornelius, is that there was never a robot war that saw billions of humans die! This is purely a construct that was developed by Wade Enterprises after their droids took over the world. It is true that one man, Edgar Wade, was responsible for the Federation – but only because he was the owner of Wade Enterprises and ordered his droid army to take over because he was power hungry!" "…", Cornelius opened his mouth to speak, but no words came out. "I know. It is a lot to take in. But you have to accept this as the honest truth, because we are going to attack the heart of Droid Central tomorrow and take back our lives." Janet paused for a moment, appreciating how difficult all of this was to take in. "The simple truth of the matter is, we need you to make our plan work!" Just like any human working for the droids, he so wanted to help, but a lifetime of fear had been instilled into him, "I am sorry, you have the wrong person! I can't get involved in this!" Janet looked at the other rebels in the room for a moment, then turned back to face him, "You don't realise it, Cornelius, but you are already involved, more deeply than you think!" A puzzled expression settled onto his face, giving Janet a chance to explain her statement. "Jacob over there was a third-class officer in droid central, just like us. He had been working there for two years, just like us, when he found out what happened to his colleague Thomas. You see, Thomas had gone missing, supposedly demoted and knocked down to the sub levels according to the droids. Jacob didn't believe this as he was very good friends with Thomas and the pair had made a pact that if either of them was demoted, the other would help. So, when Jacob hadn't heard anything from him, he investigated. He cloned a droid's security access card and looked on the mainframe for Thomas. What he found was a different story altogether. According to the mainframe, Thomas had been reassigned to section eleven of Droid Central, which, as you know, is off limits to humans. So, Jacob went there and tried to gain access using the droid's security card, but the system had picked up that the droid was in a different part of the building, so as he swiped the cloned card, the alarms went off and the building went into lockdown. He managed to hide by jumping into the trash shoot and narrowly escaped detection when he made his way out of droid central in the sub levels!" Janet paused for a moment and looked at Jacob, who was nodding along to her words. She continued after a short pause, "Since then, he has been asking questions and watching what goes on. It seems that after two years, the droid supervisors step up their complaints about the inhuman deadlines being missed by threatening pay deductions. This of course makes us work harder, which then leads them to offer us a promotion to section eleven!", she paused again, seeing the story was ringing alarm bells with Cornelius, "You see, they did the same to me, however, fortunately, Jacob had warned me about all this, one night at Agar's. Sure, I thought he was a drunken fool at first, but when they offered me a promotion to section eleven, I knew I had to run! I faked illness and was booked for an appointment at the Hospital! After that, I ran to Agar's, and I have been hiding ever since!" "Hang on a minute!", interrupted Cornelius, "So, what you are telling me is that Jacob's friend went missing but works at section eleven supposedly. Jacob, set off alarms by breaking the rules, and you just panicked and went into hiding!" "No, it's more than that. We are not the only ones!", pointing to a thin, tall, balding man, she continued, "Gary here has cracked the code! With unregistered gear from the hidden market of the sub levels, he has hacked into the central computer and found the truth... It's not just Thomas and me who have been supposedly promoted to section eleven, but every human who has ever worked there. At any one time, only three humans work on that floor, and after two years, they are transferred to section eleven, and they never leave!" Janet gestured at Gary to bring the screen over to show Cornelius, "What's more, you are scheduled to be promoted tomorrow!". He read the screen, and right enough, it stated Cornelius Crown Promotion to Section Eleven. He sat silent, wondering what he could possibly say. Instead, the previously silent Gary spoke in a high-pitched nasally voice, "This is why we need you to accept the promotion and go to sector eleven! But don't worry, because you won't be alone.", Gary held up a card sized cube, "Take this with you tomorrow and I will be able to hack the computer system inside section eleven! I will be able to gain control of the whole section, even the droids! Janet and Jacob will be waiting outside the section, so once you're in, they will join you, and we will have many more waiting in the sub levels to help!" Janet cut in on the end of Gary's words, "Tomorrow, Cornelius, we take back control!" Still somewhat taken back by everything he had heard and the zeal of the few rebels he had now met, Cornelius felt he had little choice but to go along with their exploit in the hope it would prove to be the right thing to do, "Okay, let's do this.", he agreed. After spending a few more hours going over the plan in more detail, he returned home, far more sober than he had hoped to be at that point in time. He had the cube with him, but it was inside a lead case which protected it from being discovered by the sensors around the city, in his apartment or even at Droid Central. To ensure Ezme didn't discover the secret item, he took it to bed with him and never let go of it all night.

Yesterday had been a rather trying day, and as Cornelius woke, immediately his mind was set on today's challenge. Not knowing if he would survive the attempted coup, he asked Ezme for a double portion of waffles and syrup. The usual warning about a

119

meeting with his technical supervisor was given, and an exacting specification of today's hovercar arrival was provided. He thought it odd that today, despite the madcap plan afoot, his anxiety was gone, and he felt calm. Today, he felt human and proudly walked into the hovercar when it arrived. Just as expected, his supervisor granted him a promotion and sent him downstairs to section eleven! As he took the elevator down, a few little nerves did shake within, but way less than any previous panic attack. In fact, this felt different; this was adrenaline, his body was simply preparing for a fight. Passing by the rubbish shoot, he took note of the X marked on the bottom corner, that was the sign, everything is a go, Janet and Jacob were in place. Cornelius swiped his access card, and the door to section eleven slid open. He remembered what Gary had told him: walk into the middle of the room, let the door close and then remove the lead case from the cube and wait. He took a deep breath and continued forward slowly. Ahead at the far end of the room was a reception desk where a droid sat waiting for him. He felt he was walking in slow motion as he was so conscious of every movement he made. As he neared the middle of the room, he heard the door close behind him, and he knew it was time, and he faked a trip and pretended to stumble over. At this point, he slipped off the lead case before he stood back up and dusted himself off. Count to twenty before moving,

Gary had told him, so he stood there, silently in the middle of the room, counting, "...one, two, three, four...", "What is going on?", enquired the droid from behind the desk. "Five, six, seven, eight, nine...", "Why are you standing still?", the droid continued, sounding increasingly alarmed. "Ten, eleven, twelve, thirteen...", "Something is wrong! Must apprehend and interrogate!", spoke the droid who had started moving out from behind the desk. "Fourteen, fifteen, sixteen, seventeen...", "Firewalls are being breached, must apprehend human!", exclaimed the droid that was now hurtling towards Cornelius. "Eighteen, nineteen, twenty!" he counted, and still the droid came at him with its eyes illuminated red for attack. He battled against his urge to jump out of the way as the droid came at him in the hope that Gary was working his magic as he said he could. Putting all his faith in Gary, he closed his eyes and waited for the droid to make contact! A moment later, when no contact was made, he opened his eyes again to find the droid had stopped one inch away from him and powered down. Moments later, the door slid open behind, and both Janet and Jacob entered. "Awesome job, mate!" commended Jacob as he walked past Cornelius and patted him on the back. "We don't have any time to waste, the peacekeepers operate on a separate programme to the standard droids, we need to turn off their programme from the inner lab! Come on, let's move!", ordered Janet as she too patted Cornelius on the back, "The lab should be just ahead through the next set of doors. The doors also ran on a different programme, and an access card had to be retrieved from the lifeless droid in the middle of the room before they could get them open. "Scherump", went the door as it slid open, letting the team into the main laboratory. As they turned a corner, the main computer access was dead ahead of them on a module about five feet from the glass which separated the controllers from the laboratory floor. Janet made a beeline for the module and started entering the override and shutdown codes that Gary spoke to her through the earpiece she was wearing. As she did, both Jacob and Cornelius approached the windows and looked upon the laboratory floor. As they stood and stared, their faces dropped as a horrific sight met their eyes. It was a sight too brutal, too horrific for words. All Jacob could manage was, "Janet, look!" As Janet's attention was averted from her task, and she saw with her own eyes, she let out a short shriek! Ahead of the three lay a laboratory, come factory floor, which hosted row upon row of operating tables. Each table held what was once a captive human, each operated upon to varying levels and more machine now than human. They all looked dead to the world, apart from an eerie red glow that emanated from the empty space where their eyes had once lived. "It's an

army!", voiced Cornelius. "Have you entered
the codes, Janet?" asked the disembodied
voice of Gary through her earpiece. "Shit, the
codes!", she said out loud as she refocused
on the job she was tasked with. It would take
her another minute of typing to complete. The
bad news was that the peacekeepers had
already noticed their droid counterparts had
ceased to operate, and they were headed right
for the main laboratory to investigate. Gary
picked up the movement on his scanners, but
hid the information from the team, for he
knew that Janet needed to be focused rather
than panicked. Half a minute later, the droids
were only four levels below. Having to use the
stairs had slowed them down, but if Janet
didn't complete the code entry that Gary was
reading out, well, it would be all in vain.
"They are starting to move!" announced
Jacob as he saw the half-robotic and half-
flesh fingers start to move on the cyborgs.
"They are activating!" agreed Cornelius.
Despite a quick glance up, Janet continued to
type. In the laboratory, the cyborgs had
climbed down off their tables and had started
moving towards the control room. "Hurry up,
Janet! Jacob shouted; his automatic rifle
ready to fire. Janet felt the panic of the
situation, but Gary reassured her, and she
continued typing. "Nearly there now, Janet,
keep going!" he affirmed to her as he read off
the last line of code. In that moment, the
cyborgs reached the control room and moved
towards them all. Some of them limped,

others crawled as they were all in various stages of completion, but all existed as hideous monsters outside of the laws of nature. Janet finished entering the code and ran to the others, who were all now backed into a corner, watching the painful advance. "The code will take a moment to work!" warned Gary as Jacob started firing at the creatures as they advanced towards them. Clunking from the other room announced the entry of the peacekeeper droids, and they knew they were all done for, unless that code worked quickly!

Blood of the Grail

"Dr Green", called a stern-sounding voice from across the lecture room. The smile on the previously excited and exuberant young lady disappeared, as if a puppet master had suddenly cut the strings controlling her smile. The smile she had

126

always worn unconsciously when giving a history lecture. The students called her Giggle Green or, less frequently, Dr Giggles for this very reason. Despite creating these nicknames in fun, her students regarded Dr Green warmly and always enjoyed her lectures. The smile had disappeared as she realised that distant voice was not from one of her keen students, but from one of two police men standing just inside the doorway of the lecture theatre. "Are you Dr Green?" the follow-up question came. "Well, erm... Yes, yes, I am", answered Dorothy, taken slightly aback by this break from the usual. "We need you to come with us immediately!" stated the man walking towards her whilst holding an official-looking badge in front of him. As the man spoke, Tania, a fellow lecturer, entered the theatre, "I will finish the lecture, Dr Green". Unknowing whether she was suspected of some form of foul play or not. Quickly racking her mind for any memories of unlawful behaviour to no avail. "Perhaps, it is about a student of mine!" she thought as she gingerly picked up her things and walked over to the men. The man who spoke previously held his badge out for approval. She looked at the badge carefully to make it appear she knew what she was doing, all the time thinking to herself that she had no way of knowing if it was real. If it were an ancient Egyptian Scarab, she could identify its authenticity, but this police badge could be out of a packet of cereal for all she knew. "Mmm...", she said and nodded approval to the officer. "Where are you taking me? I am booked to give lectures all afternoon." "You have been called to attend a COBR meeting at Whitehall in two hours. There is no time to waste. We have a helicopter outside waiting to take you to Edinburgh Airport, where a private jet will take you to London." "Why me? What could I possibly say at a COBR meeting? Does the Prime Minister need an ancient Egyptian relic valuation?" she asked jokingly. "We don't know Dr Green; it's above our pay grade!" A million thoughts cascaded across her conscious brain as to the reason behind this urgent request. It is true that the good doctor was working on a matter of great historical importance. One which, if she was right, would cause every history book to be rewritten, but surely, the emergence of human history was not a concern for an emergency meeting in Whitehall! 'No!', she thought, as a fleeting thought implanted a crazy friend and colleague popped to the front of her grey matter. Not unless ancient aliens really did build the pyramids and have since infiltrated governments of the world, controlling everyone's fate in a shadowy game of secrecy! She shook the thought from her head. Remembering the vast amount of laboratory-made whiskey Ted had been drinking, when at a university function, he had made a point of telling her his lengthy and drunken ramblings about government conspiracies and aliens living amongst us. For a second, the good doctor's smile came back, as she laughed at herself for contemplating his theory. "I can't go to London! Are you mad? I have Shelley to look after!" "Oh, we had it on record that you lived alone, there was no mention of a child.", said the puzzled officer.

"You have a file on me, what am I, a terrorist now?" she said rather angrily. "They have a file on everyone dear, even me.", the other older officer added. "Well, that is unethical and plainly wrong. And I am not your dear, you can call me Doctor Green, as I worked long and hard for that title." "So sorry, doctor, I didn't mean to offend." Having quickly calmed and realised she was lashing out a little at the poor officer, she replied, "No, I'm sorry, I was taken back a little, that's all. Shelley is not my child, but my dog, and he will need feeding and walking." "Dr, I would be personally happy to take care of Shelley in your absence. I do have a fondness for dogs myself. He will be safe with me, Doctor Green." She thought for a moment, and on realising that she couldn't very well turn down the Prime Minister's invitation, she agreed to the officer's kind offer. "Here is my flat key, there is special food in the cupboard for Shelley. Please do not give him anything else to eat as HE is on a strict diet and needs to be gluten free." "I will look after him, doctor!" the officer confirmed. "Can I ask, is he Coeliac?" Sudden relief flooded across her face in knowing the officer knew about Coeliac disease. "Yes, he is Officer McNab. I saved him from a dog rescue; they were about to put him down as he was very poorly. I took him home, and a friend of mine from the university ran some tests and found out. He is so much better now." "My daughter is coeliac, she has long since left home, mind, but I do understand," said Officer McNab. "I feel so much happier knowing that, thank you. There is one more thing you should know, Shelley only has three legs, but he is very good on them." "Don't fret, I will take good care of him for as long as you are gone; it will be my pleasure. I will head over there straight away." Ingrained with a new fondness for Officer McNab, she couldn't help but give this kindly man a hug before she was escorted to the car waiting for her. "Thank you."

The trip through the town was quick due to the time of day; everyone was busy at work and not on the road, causing the usual traffic jams she always experienced on her journey to and from the university every day. Strangely, they drove to the nearby hospital, which struck Doctor Green as very odd, until she realised it was simply for access to the helipad. There sat a police helicopter with its rotor blades still spinning, as the police car pulled up. As they got out of the car, another officer told them they needed to be quick, as an accident patient was expected inbound in ten minutes, so they hurried the doctor aboard. Her last time on board a helicopter had been in 2018 during the RAP (Rare Artefact Project). A project she had led supposedly in search of ancient Egyptian artefacts, which were rumoured to have been relocated across the Mediterranean and the African Continent. It hadn't been exactly the truth, but knowing she needed to tempt potential investors with the idea of fame in finding lost treasures, she had exaggerated the real aim of the research. In all fairness, some lost treasures were found at the most southernmost tip of Africa, which the doctor had brought back to the UK to be displayed at the British Museum. The true reason for the exploration was really quite a different matter. Based on a little-known tablet found in the tomb of a high-ranking official of ancient Egypt and the doctor's very own private deciphering of the text, she believed that some form of important ancient journey had occurred from South Africa by a person described to be Ra, the sun God of the ancient Egyptians. The text described this God's journey ending in water, which, as the tablet described, 'put out the fire of the God's chariot'. By the doctors' calculations, this journey would have occurred at approximately the time when the first examples of human writings occurred. She had thought that perhaps, due to the appearance of these first human tablets, that maybe a significant astrological event had grasped the imagination of those early humans and been some form of precursor in human development. Surely, she thought, if ancient humans had witnessed a comet burn through the atmosphere and make landfall in a body of water, then this may have inspired ancient mankind to dream and develop outside of the mundane. Such a theory would have been laughed at by her peers and the establishment, which is why Doctor Green had only spoken about this with Shelley and secretly created such an elaborate project to fund her research. Another thought had struck her: was her removal of the artefacts from South Africa now the reason behind this emergency meeting? She was very aware of the growing importance paid to the repatriation of museum artefacts that had technically been stolen from other countries. The Benin Bronzes being a prime example. She wouldn't know until she was in the meeting, but one thing was guaranteed: she would worry about this throughout the whole trip now.

Dorothy remembered how anxious she had felt before securing investors for her project. Initially, she had considered being truthful about her intentions, 'state some geographical info about the trip. I.e., this landscape feature, etc, and squeeze in and around information about her findings during the project, to give the idea that Ra had supposedly travelled in a golden wind chariot over South Africa, etc, in a direct line to the Dead Sea. Explain how this is reported in carvings, wall paintings and numerous decorated artefacts found specifically in locations across Africa along what is nearly a direct line pointing towards the southern part of the Dead Sea,' she thought. It all seemed to add up. Imagining herself being ousted from academia amongst jeers and laughter, she decided to focus upon the path of decorated artefacts that had been found and insist this meant many artefacts still waited to be found in underexplored locations along this path! Her plan had worked, and the watered-down version of the truth had gained her all the funding she had needed. More artefacts were found, all indicating that, certainly, a golden or fiery bright object was recorded along what is nearly a straight path stretching from across Africa. This meant the most logical body of water this comet could have struck was not the River Nile, as she had first imagined from that mind-bending tablet, but the Dead Sea. Sadly, the good doctor's theory had fallen completely apart at this stage, as all her research showed no evidence of a crater along the supposedly witnessed path of the comet. Maybe she had seen only what she wanted to see, maybe it had only existed in her head. Such a finding would have been revolutionary, to be able to point at one event in pre-history and just say, that is where it all began, and Dr Dorothy Green being credited with discovering it. Now that would have been something; instead, all the good doctor was left with were more questions and no answers. As she sat in a police car being transported across London, 'One day,' she thought, 'one day I will get more funding and look again.'

The COBR meeting started and the Prime Minister addressed the various ministers, "You will notice that we have a rather unusual guest joining us today,", the Prime Ministered gestured towards doctor Green and everyone turned towards her as he continued, "Dr Dorothy Green has been given the highest security clearance in respect of all matters involved in today's meeting.", he paused for a moment as if collecting his thoughts, his expression gave nothing away as seen in so many long term politicians who have developed hardened poker faces through the keeping of governmental secrets. The Prime Minister faced to look directly at Dorothy, "In my position as Prime Minister, I thank you for agreeing to attend today's meeting." Turning to the rest of the room, "We have followed the work of Dr Green carefully, and whether she realises it or not, it runs in parallel to our current concerns." Dorothy was overwhelmed as she struggled to understand the Prime Minister's vague introduction. "Dr Green, as I said, our government has taken a great interest in your work and let me begin by saying that every site you visited during your Rare Artefacts Project has also been visited and documented by our service! It has been surmised that your Project was a front you used to gain funding for your own separate research, research you have kept secret" Mind blown, was an understatement as Dorothy sat still, red-faced and taken aback by the amount of knowledge gained about her. Her mind worked fast, soon realising that nothing yet had been stated and all this was simply hearsay scratching upon a brick wall between her secret theory and her visits to Africa. "That's quite okay, Dr Green, I do not expect you to tell us about your private research, at least, not yet. Not until you have heard about our current concerns, then I hope you may be in a position to help us move forward. We have tea, coffee, and some snacks you can help yourself to. I realise you have already had rather an unexpected long day, and this is a very foreign situation for you to find yourself in. So, we will take a fifteen-minute break now for you to get settled and collect your thoughts before we begin." With that, the Prime Minister left the room, followed by every other minister, leaving but one member of staff to keep Dorothy company. "Would you like a cup of Tea?" he asked to prompt Dorothy into action. "Errm, Yes, I suppose..." The gentleman immediately moved towards the table containing the refreshments, "How do you like your Tea, Dr Green?", "Milk and one sugar please" "Very well, shall I bring over a small assortment of snacks, this meeting is likely to take a number of hours, doctor?", "Oh, that sounds lovely, thank you so much." The truth of the matter was that

Dorothy was starving and hadn't had any lunch today, with all the commotion, and was truly grateful for these offerings. She had already devoured a croissant before the delegation re-entered the room. Despite attempting to be extra careful and not make a mess of crumbs, some now stuck to her jumper's sleeve, which, thankfully, she was unaware of. "Miss, sorry, Dr Green, you will find a notepad and pen in front of you, for any notes you may wish to make. I know this is all very strange for you, and I am very pleased to see you have taken the opportunity to get something to eat and drink. What will happen now is a presentation of our current situation and what we know will be given, then at the end, I will ask you if you have any questions or have anything to add, which may help." With that, the Prime Minister sat down, and one of the ministers stood up and beckoned for the lights to be dimmed and the projector to be turned on. He pulled up a picture of great devastation in South Africa. This is a picture of Cape Town taken today following the most recent earthquake to affect the region. So far, it is estimated that two thousand people may be trapped, injured or dead. He clicked the button, and a picture of a flooded town appeared. Here is the town of Gansbaai. A seismic-activated landslide at Enderby Land caused a tsunami that flooded this town. Sadly, the loss of life from this event was estimated at over three thousand,

and the local agriculture and economy were decimated. This photograph was taken three days ago. Another click of his button displayed a further horror of nature. Here is the southern coast of the African continent. As you can see, the southern coast has been completely destroyed" The picture showed hundreds of broken and overturned boats and ships along the coast, with city after city wiped out. "The estimated loss of life is around eight million, and the cost of damage is unprecedented. This photograph was taken three hours ago." The man clicked again, but this time a map appeared instead of painful photographs of devastation. "From our perspective, it seems obvious we have entered an era of increased seismic activity. For the United Kingdom, we must look to the past to understand what threats may lie in the future. We have developed a false sense of safety regarding threats, as they are rather uncommon occurrences for us. However, the threat does exist, and we must be aware of this. In 1858, a tsunami was reported by witnesses in England, Germany, the Netherlands and Denmark. Significant flooding occurred in the west of England on the same day. "Another click brought up an old, inked sketch of ships sinking. "In 1580, a 5.8 magnitude earthquake with its epicentre in the seabed near Calais caused giant waves. Hundreds of people were killed when ships sank, and low-lying coastal land was inundated by the sea. Part of Dover Cliff collapsed, taking with it part of Dover Castle" "Of course, there have been many more incidents such as this throughout our history. Further to this, we must also realise that quite a large proportion of the UK is low-lying and largely unprepared for such occurrences. Geologists have found a number of likely ways tsunamis could occur, causing widespread devastation to the UK." Another click pulled up a photograph of a volcano, "This is the Cumbre Vieja Volcano in La Palma, just off North Africa, it has been identified as the greatest potential risk to Great Britain due to the instability of the volcano and expectation that a future eruption will cause a huge mass of rock to break off and fall into the sea, in turn generating a huge tsunami surge in the Atlantic Ocean. The wave would strike Spain, Portugal, the east coast of the United States, France, the southern and western parts of Ireland and the south coast of England. The wave would take six hours to reach us, with estimates of a wave to be at a height of ten metres when it does. Britain's estimated loss of life is in the thousands." After a short pause in silence, the minister thanked the Prime Minister and sat down. The room was now silent, and Dorothy started to see how the issues featured along areas she had researched, but could not see any value or real connection to her research. The Prime Minister stood up, "Thank you, Minister, for a well-explained presentation. I think I can speak for everyone here today that we now understand the considerable potential danger of an increase in seismic activity for the United Kingdom. I understand, too, that you picked just a handful of occurrences from history, when there have been many more than you mentioned. A substantial landslide of material from any one of a number of locations could have a devastating effect."

"Could the ministry of defence please now give an outline of what we factually know about the other seemingly interlinked occurrences please" As the Prime Minister sat down, a grey determined man stood up and walked to the projector screen, "May I remind everyone, especially Dr Green that everything said in this room is top secret and repeating this information outside this room is treason and punishable under British law as such..." He clicked the button, and a map of the globe appeared. "We have, for the past week, been studying a rather strange phenomenon. One week ago, our military picked up low-frequency waves originating from the area of the Dead Sea." A click of his button made the map centre on the Dead Sea, and a ring appeared at the apparent transmission location. "Now, low-frequency waves can travel very far, which is why they were picked up. Low-frequency waves are also fairly harmless to the environment. In the early hours of today, we picked up a second source of low-frequency waves". He clicked the button again, and Dorothy's head exploded into realms of the improbable. "This is Dronning Maud Land in the Antarctic, 2400 miles from the south coast of Africa. What is more, on further analysis, it has been found that both this site in Antarctica and the site in the Dead Sea are also emitting a higher frequency. The higher frequencies we feel are triggering the seismic activity being experienced. The south coast of Africa has been devastated by a huge Tsunami caused by a huge landslide from Enderby Land in the Antarctic. Further loss of life and devastation is expected in India and Japan in the coming hours, and we have joined other nations in a huge evacuation effort. We can only pray it is in time." The Prime Minister introduced the next speaker, "This is Dr Alberts, he is the head of our in-house scientific community. For the benefit of Dr Green, I must advise that Dr Alberts has been the lead man in examining the Dr.'s research.", "Thank you Prime Minister. Dr Green, I do apologise, I feel quite awkward talking about your research when you will certainly be able to clarify things far better than I, so please bear with me." The projector now changed to a map of Africa, which showed the sites Dr Green had investigated. "These are the sites in Africa that Dr Green investigated under her Rare Artefacts Project. It all seemed rather innocent and ordinary on first examination. However, in time, we came to note that each location held a similarity that no one expected." He clicked the button, and the next slide of the projector blew away any doubts Dorothy had about being in the wrong place. "This image is a cave painting which shows, for all intents and purposes, an unidentified glowing object in the sky. The next image is another interpretation of the same, this time carved into wood. The next image shows an early piece of pottery with similar imagery. In fact, every single one of these sites hold this connection through various images. We do not understand their value, but what we found is rather peculiar, that is, when we draw a straight line between these sites, if we extend it at the up most region", he clicks the button again and the map zooms out and extends the upper part of the line, "this line links up with the source of the high and low frequencies in the Dead Sea. This, we may think, on its own, is pure coincidence. However, if we then extend the bottom of the line," another click now extends the bottom part of the line on the projector screen, "we can see quite clearly that this line passes extremely close to the source of the same problems in the Antarctic, and that cannot be a coincidence." The Prime Minister stood up, "Thank you, Dr Alberts, I thank you and everyone else for doing an excellent job of bringing us all up to speed. I am fairly sure, that you will have your own questions doctor Green, you will certainly now know how much of your work we have guessed about and I hope you may be able to offer some indication about what you were searching for and what led you on this search with your project, as it does currently seem inexplicably linked to the current disaster facing our planet. The floor is yours, Dr Green." Dorothy stood up, still shocked by the revelations she had heard. She walked over to the projector. "Can you pull up that last slide again, please?" The slide appeared on the screen, showing the line her work followed. She thought for a moment and then spoke, "My work was based on my own deciphering of the Umdo tablet. As I read this tablet, it told me of a recorded event, about the God Ra, who travelled across Africa in a golden chariot. This journey is described as ending in water, which put out the fire from the God's chariot. My theory, which I think may now have been wrong, was that a comet had crossed the sky and come to earth, landing in a body of water, I noticed that around the time of this record, that human recording and writing took off, and I felt that witnessing this comet had ignited a desire to learn and imagine. I searched Africa for any evidence, under the guise of my project. My thought was that the comet may have landed in the River Nile; however, as my findings show here, the path of what I thought was a comet led to the Dead Sea. However, I was never able to find an impact crater, and my research stalled until today. Now it seems clear to me that something flew from one location to the other. This all sounds crazy, but can I ask if an impact crater has been detected in Antarctica?" The room fell silent, so the Prime Minister prompted an answer, "We are all on the same team here. Dr Alberts, has an impact crater been found in Antarctica?"

"In complete honesty, we had not even considered looking, Sir." "Very well, how do we check for one?" asked the Prime Minister. Dorothy felt much more confident and offered an answer, "We need satellite images, Prime Minister, that show the density of the rock in the area. If there has been an impact, then we will see a ring evident around the impact." "Thank you, Dr Green. I feel that you are already leading us in a new direction, as I had hoped you would. Right, we will have a half-hour break now, whilst the Ministry of Defence and Dr Alberts find an appropriate image for us to check for an impact crater. I thank everyone for their efforts, and I do think we are on the verge of a breakthrough that we must credit Dr Green with."

With the room empty once more, Dorothy tucked into another croissant as her mind ran rampant with multiple scenarios. A comet had seemed the only logical solution, at least, it had, until the news about the generation of low and high frequencies came. Now, astrological events made no sense at all! With a quick internet search, Dorothy found that nature can emit low frequencies through earthquakes, thunder, waterfalls and even ocean waves. But none of that tied in with the current situation as had been explained today. In the quiet, Dorothy's mind travelled back to the echoing hallways of Cairo's Egyptian Museum, where she had stood transfixed by photographs of ancient cave paintings in Mali, West Africa. She remembered thinking of how the intricate, otherworldly designs seemed to tell a story that spanned continents and eras. As an archaeologist with a fascination for mythological creatures, Dorothy, in her younger days, had dedicated her life to understanding the origins of the beings that haunted humanity's oldest legends. Little did she know the Umdo tablet was a further stepping stone along her journey. Having taken her from the scorching sands of Egypt across little-explored parts of Africa to the southernmost tip. Never had she thought of venturing further south to the icy desolation of Antarctica. Sat alone with her thoughts, she questioned what exactly may lie undisturbed under the frozen tundra of Antarctica! Of what secrets lay in wait, that would change everything she thought she knew about mankind's history! Dorothy's research had led her to uncover striking similarities between the cave paintings in Africa, the hieroglyphics in Egypt, and the frescoes of ancient Greece. Each depicted figures that were unmistakably mythological: Minotaurs, Sphinxes, Centaurs, and the towering Nephilim. Now her mind ran wild with crazy, never-to-be-spoken-of thoughts, and she hypothesised that these creatures were not mere figments of human imagination but the result of ancient alien experiments. Her crazy thoughts were thankfully interrupted as the ministers filed back into the room, followed moments later by the Prime Minister, who asked for an update. Dr Alberts pulled up a geological map of Antarctica and explained that the image showed that no crater existed, which meant the comet theory did not hold water. "However, if we look at the latest satellite image of the area.", Dr Albert paused and clicked on to the next image he had set up. "We can see here, in the location we have pinpointed as the origin of the frequencies, there has been some form of subsidence or cave-in!" The image showed a wide hole in a section of snow-covered landscape. "What is more interesting is what we see if we enlarge this image!" A click made it happen, and what appeared to be a reflective metal surface became just visible deep within the hole. The room fell silent, only interrupted, eventually, by the Prime Minister. "Dr Albert, do we know what we are looking at, or how long it has been there?" "Quite frankly, Prime Minister, no, we don't! Our satellites do not fly directly above the Antarctic, so we can only capture such highly angled images. However, it is obvious that some form of metallic object is at the bottom of that hole. As for how long it has been there, well, all I can confirm is it must have been there for thousands of years, judging by previous satellite imagery, which shows a gradual uncovering of this object!" The doctor clicked through a series of images from the past five years that showed the hole gradually forming and exposing what lies beneath. The room fell silent again until Dorothy picked up the courage to express her interest. "With respect, Prime Minister, may I suggest leading an expedition to this anomaly to explore the connection it holds to my work and all that has been said today!" She felt her heart beating quicker than usual as she spoke, partly from being out of place in these surroundings, but mainly out of excitement to finally get to the bottom of her research. "Thank you for your help today. Doctor Green, could I ask you to kindly leave the room for a moment whilst I speak with my ministers concerning this matter." Dorothy was escorted out of the room to a waiting area, where she was brought a further cup of tea. An hour later, the ministers left the meeting, and some seemed rather unhappy with whatever had been discussed in her absence. Finally, the Prime Minister exited the room along with Dr Albert, and they both walked over to Dorothy. "Doctor Green, you will be pleased to learn that I concur with your suggestion of an expedition being led to the Antarctic. Further, despite some disapproval by my ministers, I have decided that you will lead this expedition alongside Doctor Albert, and a pre-selected team to support and secure this expedition!" Dorothy smiled to know her research would hopefully finally become complete, "Thank you, Prime Minister!" she replied. "Don't thank me too fast, you have a great ordeal ahead of you, and your flight to Argentina leaves in three hours, so there is little time to waste. Please confer with Dr Albert now to ensure you have all the equipment needed for your expedition." The Prime Minister then left, and Dr Albert explained to Dorothy, "When he says team members to provide security, he means a few fellows from MI5! A few ministers felt this must be terrorist activity and wanted to drop a bomb on the site we are headed to! "Really!" answered Dorothy, taken aback by how stupid ministers could be. "It's true, I'm sorry to say. Some ministers, I have found, are rather trigger-happy, but have no fear, we are the ones leading this expedition! So, what do you think?" he asked, fishing for answers. After no response other than a shrug from Dorothy, he continued, "Based purely on the length of time under the snow, it may be related to a previously unknown civilisation of mankind. One that pre-dates all known records!", he examined Dorothy's face for any sign of intrigue and then continued, "Perhaps even ancient aliens!", he stopped there as he saw Dorothy's expression change as if she was hoping for a topic change, not wanting to let her own thoughts out for fear of ridicule. She knew her theory would likely be met with scepticism, even though her life's work now pointed them both to the most inhospitable place on Earth—the Antarctic, which would have been an ideal location for any alien craft to be hidden from man.

Braving the icy winds and treacherous terrain, Dorothy, Dr Albert and their team finally reached the edge of the hole late in the day under the dark skies of the polar night and set up camp. Tomorrow, after a good night's sleep, they would wait for the arrival of two helicopters in order to safely and quickly descend the two thousand feet to the base of the hole. Dorothy was excited, but the past thirty-six hours had been a strain with little sleep, so right now, she let her mind rest and drifted off into a deep sleep.

Travelling through a cavern made of ice and metal, as she rounded a corner, it opened up into a huge control room. At the far end, a large figure stood in a shadow that receded the closer Dorothy got to the figure. Until she stood before a giant figure whose alien features and bug-like eyes could be clearly seen. The mysterious alien stared at Dorothy, his large alien eyes piercing her soul and making her tremble with fear. Then he spoke, "I have been waiting thousands of years for your arrival, Dorothea, our saviour!" The earth started shaking around them both, and the ground lifted up, fast into the air, pushing Dorothy against the surface of what now seemed to be a spaceship! Sweat streamed off her in fear as her mind spun and the room shook more and more. Then she woke, it had only been a vivid dream, and

Dorothy lay back down in her bed, realising there were still several hours until the morning.

Morning was a weird phenomenon during the polar night, when day resembled night just as night resembled day. Thankfully, breakfast resembled bacon and eggs on toast, so everyone had a good start to their day. The group checked all the equipment the doctors had requested after breakfast, and it all checked out just fine. A seemingly endless wait for the helicopters then took over. The group only needed one helicopter, but in pre-expedition discussion with Dr Albert, it had been decided they would double up on what was required in order to avoid the deadly scenario of becoming stuck two thousand feet below the ice if the helicopter broke down.

Finally, the helicopters arrived, and after a quick refuel and check over, the group began the descent into the hole. As they descended, everyone fell speechless as the item of their investigation became clearly visible. Unearthed, from a sleep of thousands of years, lay a colossal spaceship. It had been buried beneath the ice, frozen in time. Dorothy remembered her dream as the reality of life she had known fell apart. Had it been a dream, or had live aliens communicated with her last night? Surely not, she thought. After all, no one could survive thousands of years under a frozen, lifeless tundra! The team scanned the ship for life as they descended, but it was completely devoid of any heat signatures. Upon landing, the security force took point and circled the large craft, which was about the size of a jumbo jet, checking for heat signatures and entrances to no avail. Once they had completed their scans, the all clear was given, and only then were the scientists allowed to take over. Dorothy was among the first to approach in awe and wonder. No one could understand how the ship operated or even how to gain entrance. After spending all afternoon in the hole, documenting every aspect of the ship they could see, the group left some sentry cameras in place and the helicopter took them back up to camp. After a hot meal, the scientists viewed the digital photographs they had taken of the ship. Whilst they worked, the helicopters lowered laboratory modules down to the base of the hole. As they studied the images, one person who supposedly knew more about this particular field of study was Hugo Mook, a self-confessed conspiracy theorist, who, prior to being included in this expedition, had been convinced that aliens existed amongst us and were in control of the governments of the world. Even now, after seeing the spaceship with his own eyes, Dorothy had heard him pass comment that it was simply an elaborate set-up to distract attention from how the governments were controlling people's actions by television-induced thought control! Some of the team had started calling him Spooky Mooky;

however, Dorothy had brought about a quick end to that when she openly chastised them without a second thought. Quite rightly too, in her mind. After all, this was a professional expedition of great urgency, and that made everyone responsible for behaving professionally and not like children. In truth, she had received many taunts growing up and felt Hugo's pain. Besides, despite how crazy his ideas may have seemed previously, right now, he was the only person here who had ever believed in alien activity. He was the only one who had researched this stuff, and right now, that made him a valuable member of the team. Hugo looked closely over the images that had been taken, looking for any marks or indicators that he had seen or heard tales of before. Eventually, after hours of looking, it was Hugo who made the first breakthrough. "It's writing! Instructions!" he exclaimed excitedly and rather loudly to the group. "What, don't be stupid! That means nothing!", retorted Christina, who was one of Dr Albert's students, and maybe not so incidentally one of the team who had been verbally shut down by Dorothy earlier for name-calling. "It is, I tell you, it is instructions!" Hugo stated. "Okay then, what do they say?" came back another sarcastic reply by Christina. "I don't speak alien. How am I meant to know what it says? Perhaps it says unleaded only!" Christina laughed at Hugo, trying to put him down. "Let me have a look, Hugo. This may be the breakthrough we need!" Dorothy hoped her words would put an end to the childish comments of Christina and just hoped that Hugo had actually found something of use. "Certainly, Dr Green", Hugo said with a smile, feeling a little chivvied up for her faith in his work. He brought her the screen that showed what he had identified as writing, and Dorothy's face lit up. "My goodness, you're right, Hugo! This is writing. I can't quite decipher it, but it is of a very similar style to that of the tablet of Umdo!" She fell silent as any final lingering doubts about how her work linked up to this alien spaceship were lost for good. "Send me a copy of this image, I want to study this and see if I can unlock its meaning!" said Dorothy before she retired to her quarters. For most of the night, she studied that image, deciphering a bit here and there, based on her previous research and studies. From what she could see, the writing she deciphered from the tablet of Umdo was a more modern version of this style of writing. She had cracked the code of the Umdo tablet by having a basic understanding of everything Earth-based, which meant she had a starting point of reference. In stark contrast, this inscription was understandably more alien in its style. Of course, this made complete sense as this spaceship was not from planet Earth! By the end of the night, she had deciphered only a quarter of the writing, which only told the team that "light force" held some relevance. The next day, Dr

Green informed the team of her findings. Everyone scratched their heads to try and figure out what this meant or what significance it held, if any. However, no one could figure that out. At least, not until they returned to the ship and looked at the inscription with their own eyes! They stood surrounding the panel, trying to bridge the alien gap in their knowledge. Hugo joked to himself, "Use the force!", making fun of the alien's abilities from the movies! Then his face changed from being light-hearted and silly to being deadly serious as he looked a few feet above the inscription. "Yes! That's it, yes!" he said out loud. "What is it, Hugo?" enquired the good doctor, who remained as puzzled as ever. "Use the force!" He repeated, and everyone simply repeated the same puzzled look. "Don't you get it? We need to use the force. Electric force!", he pointed up a few feet above the inscription, at what appeared suddenly to be some kind of alien socket of the card reader. "It is instructions saying to use electricity to open a door!". Everyone's mouths opened in shock as they realised that Hugo, the craziest member of the team, was right. With the change in direction Hugo had provided, the scientist team had a platform setup and started poking and prodding the socket, connecting wires up and taking readings.

The week went by slowly, as the analysis of the ship's electrical port continued slowly—too slowly for Dorothy, but she knew too well about being patient. After all, archaeology was a slow pursuit, limited by what you unearthed and the digging, which took time. All research takes time, so she waited.

Eventually, on the seventh morning, the scientists cracked the system and along with a hiss of steam and smoke, a door opened on the side of the craft. The doorway was about twelve feet high, and images flew across everyone's imagination of giant aliens, twelve feet tall. It made sense to some that aliens would be large due to the reduced gravity in space. The security force immediately surrounded the opening with guns drawn and held their station until a small number of them had got into protective suits and entered the ship. Dr Green was at base camp and watched a live feed from the security team's chest cams as they explored the vessel. It seemed derelict, and two hours of repeated searches proved this to be true. Only then were Dr Green and the scientists allowed to board the ship. It was empty, but far from dead, as it hummed with energy. There were no desiccated remains of alien pilots, but on the control deck, they saw large seats where they had once sat. In front of alien-sized seats, controls stood remaining illuminated and waiting for the expert touch of ancient alien guidance to instruct the ship. Scientists had less of a clue about what anything meant here. I guess opening a door takes somewhat less experience than controlling a spaceship! Dr Green, who felt she was truly living within a science fiction novel now, ran her hand gently over the pilot's console, as if a simple touch would somehow inspire her. Suddenly, her hand froze still! She hadn't stopped, but her hand had. She tried moving away, but her hand was held fast by some strange, unforgiving force above a circle. "Help!" she screamed, and everyone turned to see the predicament she was in. A weird bubble of energy expanded from the base of the circle and formed a perfect dome over the good doctor's hand. Hugo pulled at her hand, but it would not move. Red lights flashed on the console ahead of the bubble, just before the centre section of the circle opened up and a needle protruded upwards towards her hand. Dorothy's eyes widened in fear, her hand was completely numb, but this did not stop her from screaming as the alien medical equipment broke the skin of her index finger! It was nothing but a pin prick, and once a drop of blood settled on the end of the needle, the whole mechanism once more withdrew out of sight, and Dorothy's hand was freed. Immediately, full feeling returned as the energy bubble released its grip. "What was that about?" she asked, holding her hand to her chest as if to protect it from any more attacks. "They are sampling your blood. I reckon they are checking your DNA to see if you belong here! We need to get out now!", warned Hugo. "Agreed!" said the head of the security force. "Everyone out now!" he shouted. As he did, the pilot's chair changed shape, adjusting from that of a giant-sized seat to a regular human size. "Hang on!" spoke Hugo, "It's okay, they have accepted her. Look, the ship is changing to meet her needs!" He was right, the flashing red lights turned green, and a display lit up directly ahead of the pilot's seat. "No one sits down!" warned the captain, "No one sits down, and no one touches anything, just look. I don't want to take a trip to Mars just yet!" he jested seriously. Looking at the display, they could see a circle which looked like it represented Earth. There was a further line which came in from off the screen and travelled down the south pole, where presumably the ship landed. But then a further line traced up to what everyone could see was approximately the location of the Dead Sea. "They landed here and took a smaller shuttle to the Dead Sea!" Dorothy said, suddenly understanding everything that she had seen, heard and felt. "They came for help!" she ventured, and everyone turned to look at her, waiting for a further explanation of that last comment. "How do you know they came for help?" asked Hugo. "I don't, I just have a feeling!" said Dorothy, not wanting to say it was due to her dream! After the strange blood taking incident, it was decided that everyone should leave the ship, and Dr Green had to be isolated under quarantine for 24 hours, just to ensure she hadn't been exposed to any alien virus that might cause her to mutate into a five-headed monster set on destroying the human race! Along with a security force and medical personnel, she was held in a medical bay of the newly erected laboratory next to the spaceship.

That night, as Dorothy slept, her dreams were once again invaded by thoughts and images not of her own, but those of ancient aliens asking for help. Unbeknownst to Dorothy, she shared a special link to the ancient aliens. It was a link that had driven her work for many years, an unconscious pull that guided her every step. Even now, in her sleep, the ancient spaceship communicated telepathically with her subconscious, driving weird but informative dreams across her mind. In her dream, she was on a foreign planet. The red surface resembled her imaginings of Mars despite having never seen the planet. She somehow just knew it was Mars. There lay a vast city, hidden underground away from the radiation that bombarded the surface and had destroyed the once beautiful lakes, mountains and grassy meadows that had existed above. Through her connection to the ship, she saw images of how Mars had been much like the Earth and how life in its various guises had once prospered upon the surface. Life had needed to find new ways to exist, and huge underground cities had been constructed upon a scale no one would have imagined. They had survived, at least for a very long time, but then illness had struck them down. The radioactivity which poisoned the surface had eventually, after thousands of years, affected them, causing a degenerative blood disease. This had killed millions, and their scientists struggled to find a cure. Images of mass graves flooded her mind, as the ship spelt out in graphic detail the devastation caused. It had been a painfully sad period of Martian history, but in a vain attempt to survive, a planet-wide effort was made and the entire civilisation was placed into cryopods, to sleep in perfect stasis until a cure could be found. Those who remained awake set off upon missions across the known universe to search for a cure. This was the story of the ancient aliens who had come to Earth. They had found the DNA of early humans resembled their own makeup, and without meaning to cause any harmful side effects, they experimented on mankind in a desperate bid to cure their degenerative blood disease. As Dorothy was taken deeper into the ship's archives, it was revealed that she herself was the crowning glory of this experimentation. Flashes of information traced a line from the first experiments, which had generated larger-than-life ancestors that pre-history had regarded as the Nephilim. Hybrid beings were fashioned by combining human and Martian DNA. Footage filled Dorothy's mind as she saw mankind rewrite such scientific evolution into mythology. Of how the results of early experiments had become creatures of legend, such as the Sphinx, Minotaur and the Cyclops. She was informed how they had worked to create a cure before the aliens themselves had died. How, via remote viewing, the ship's computer had noted a sacred bloodline! A bloodline which had since been passed down over the centuries and always recorded inaccurately in human history. For the Bible held that Jesus was the son of God, whilst mankind lived oblivious to the real hands at work. Mary Magdalene had been the wife of Jesus, and through their daughter Sarah, the sacred bloodline was continued. Dorothy had heard about the notion that the bloodline of Christ was sacred and protected in secrecy even through to modern times. However, even the best stylings of fiction writers could not capture the whole truth of this significance, or how this all related directly to Dorothy. An alien voice spoke inside her head, "Dorothia, you carry within you a gift, you are the saviour of all Mars!"

As the dream finished, Dorothy came too, finding herself alone in the dark of the spaceship. She was sitting in the pilot's seat, and her hands rested upon the controls. Trying to understand how she had ended up aboard the ship, she was simply unable to appreciate that she had walked in her sleep, guided by the call of the ship. Nor could she know the ship had unlocked abilities deep within her, and with such, she had sent the entire security force and medical staff to sleep, as she passed through the new facility and out towards the ship. A calmness fell over her as she sat with her hands on the controls. The spaceship vibrated with ever increasing power and started to rise into the air. Dorothy felt at home, consumed by one thought, 'I am the saviour, this is meant to be!'

Children of Adikia

The mist silently rolled back as dawn broke, leaving its dew upon the tired old walls of the now collapsed and open parts of the mine. Slowly, thin, weak children crawled out from the shallow trenches where they had sheltered through the cold of the night. These children belonged to the Adikia, a dark entity that had stolen them away from their parents in order to satisfy its own needs. You see, for a millennium, the creature had extended his life by feasting upon a rare essence, which could be found in the narrow mines of Siphnos. Only small children could fit along the narrow passages of the mine, so he brought them here to retrieve his precious essence from deep below. In payment for their toils, he allowed them to live, providing barely sufficient food for such. He liked to snatch children as young as five years old and preferred the boys as they were stronger and more suited to the arduous work deep within the dark mine. Artemis was one such boy who had been snatched along with his twin sister Estella the day after their fifth birthday. Their parents had searched long and hard for them both without any success. After two years of holding onto hope and searching daily for any signs or clues, they had finally lost all hope. They came to believe that their beloved children must be dead, lost to the sea from the high cliffs near their home. However, despite being kept in a weakened state by the monster, they both still held a strong fire within them, which drove them and kept them alive. Not only did they have a resilience never before seen, but they also helped the weaker children, sharing their food to keep them going. Both Artemis and Estella were considered to be great champions by their fellow captives.

No one but the Adikia could travel to or from the mines of Siphnos, for such passage was only possible by travelling through an underground labyrinth where the Minotaur was imprisoned as a guardian to kill any who trod the paths of the labyrinth. Anyone, of course, except the Adikia whom the Minotaur feared. Adikia fed his mighty guardian with the flesh of the children who had grown too big to fit into the narrow mines. He would tell the children they were granted their freedom for having worked so well in the mines and set them on a path through the labyrinth. Amongst the children, rumours abounded about what happened to these freed boys and girls. Some felt they had finally found their freedom and their ways home to their families, whilst others felt it was a perilous trick of the Adikia, who had really sent them to their doom. Even those who claimed the freed children must have found their way to their homes and happiness didn't really believe their own words. But it was better to hold on to a hope that one day they too would be freed and allowed to return to their homes. To hold on to a hope that this was not the start and end of all of their young, torturous lives, but that their families waited for them gave many the strength to carry on. Artemis, on the other hand, spoke about all the children of the mines being free. He really believed it could happen. However, his sister Estella felt only gloom in their future. Still, she was determined not to lie down and die, and she always helped her brother inspire the children to keep going and silenced her own desperate feelings of doom.

Having watched Artemis show defiance so often under the Adikia's rule, the monster finally felt he must take action, worried the other children's spirits were growing and soon they would be too strong to bend under his will. For the truth was that Adikia ruled mainly by the fear he instilled into the children at a young age, his strength, although dominant, would not withstand the force of an organised rebellion of children. Therefore, fearing such a revolt could occur if he didn't act fast, he sent Artemis and his sister on their path through the labyrinth. Being amongst the youngest to ever enter the labyrinth, as they set foot upon their way to supposed freedom, they both feared that in reality their troubles may be only just beginning.

Ahead lay the gloomy entrance, much larger than the narrow child-sized tunnels of the mine. They each carried a flaming torch as they bravely made their way down the first passage of the maze. The wind carried strange noises along with it from deep within, making the torches flicker as the sound passed by their young ears. At just seven years old, both of them had experienced more suffering and hard toil than many do in an entire lifetime. Having seen friends die from weakness early on in the time they had spent in the mine, they had vowed to do whatever they could to save others from the same fate. They had shared their food often with the others, and despite having very strong spirits, their bodies were now rather frail as a consequence. Yet, they ventured onward into the dark, determined to find their way back to their home. "I'm scared!" Estella admitted as the pair heard what sounded like a growl in the distance. "That is probably just the wind, Estella. Don't worry, we have each other, it will be fine!" Artemis said in an attempt to settle his sisters' nerves. The truth, however, was that his concerns equally matched Estella's. But he knew no amount of worrying would help either of them. There was no turning back; they just had to find their way through this labyrinth. The passage split into two paths, and the duo took the right passage, hoping they had made the correct choice. Soon, they had to choose again as the passage split once more, and again, they took the right passage. They decided to take two rights and then two lefts, and so on, in the hope of being able to counter their steps if they ran into trouble. However, in no time at all, they had completely lost track of how many turns they had taken, making them lose their way within the great labyrinth. One thing which was on their side was their almost instinctive sense of direction, which they had developed over the last two years, finding their way through the dark of the mine. What was more, they could tell they were quite deep within this labyrinth by the cold and dampness of the walls and knew they must follow upward passageways to find the exit. Their progress was suddenly halted as they came upon a pit where the path had fallen away. Holding a torch low down to see the depth of the pit below, suddenly they heard snakes hiss as the light and heat emitted hurt their senses at the bottom of the pit. Some raised up, showing their fangs, were at the ready to strike anyone who came too close. Sadly, the gap was too wide for them both to jump across safely, as any miscalculation would see them fall into the pit. "We have to turn back and try another passage!" Estella said as she turned away, ready to walk back to the last intersection. "Hang on!" answered Artemis as something glinting in the torchlight caught his eye. Lying on the ground, he reached out, trying to grasp what he had seen, "I've almost got it. Hold my legs!" He stretched a little further and grasped a spear that was leaning up against the side of the pit. As he pulled on it, snakes withered below him, moving away from the disturbance, exposing the skeletal remains of the spear's previous owner, a warrior type who had fallen foul of the pit and perished, unable to escape the pit or the snakes. As the snakes escaped the light and heat, other smaller bodies became visible, and the question of what had happened to their friends was painfully answered. As Estella helped Artemis up, something else caught her eye. It was a line of thread that ran across the pit from the skeletal remains of the warrior disappearing into the darkness of the unreachable passage. "That's odd?", she said. "What's odd?" quizzed Artemis. "Look!" she said, pointing at the thread, "There is a thread running from that warrior, out of the pit and along the passage!" "That is odd. I wonder why there is a thread. Maybe he had snagged his clothing on something and had not noticed?" Estella held her torch down into the pit, and the snakes again hissed and moved away from the corpse. "No, he didn't. Look there, the thread leads from a ball of thread beside him! He put that thread down deliberately!" "But why would he do that? What would the point ...", Artemis stopped talking as a thought unwrapped a glorious answer in his mind, "Unless he came from the outside and put down that thread in order to find his way back out again!" With an excited voice, Estella added, "So, all we have to do is follow that thread and we will find our way out!" Her face then dropped again as she realised it was all useless, as they couldn't get past the pit of snakes. "Maybe, just maybe, another passage will see us come back across that thread further on! "We simply need to stay alert for it!" Artemis added, and they both felt a little happier as they turned back and took a different passage. The spear was golden and heavy to carry, but it provided the pair a bit of comfort knowing they could protect themselves against Adikia or any other monster they may come across in the dark. The duo had not travelled much further through the labyrinth when they heard a rumbling, resonant and primal growl from the passages ahead of them. Looking at each other for comfort, Artemis held up the spear as they continued to walk on a little more cautiously than before. Estella held out her torch to light the path as much as possible. Then, a deep roar ahead of them warned them of impending danger, and they both stopped and prepared themselves for an attack. In the distance of the passage, a large figure moved in the shadows and roared loudly, making them both shake. "Who dares walk my labyrinth?" growled the voice in barely understandable animalistic tones like that of a talking bear. "We are just trying to find our way out!", exclaimed Estella as Artemis strengthened his grip on the spear, readying himself to do battle. "Way out! Ha Ha Ha!" the beast laughed as he spoke, "There is no escape, no one ever leaves the Labyrinth!" Estella continued, "But please, sir, that's not true, we saw a thread leading the way out!" The beast seemed angered by this notion, "I am the Minotaur, imprisoned in this labyrinth. There is no thread, there is no way out!". "We have seen the thread running out from the pit with snakes in. We couldn't follow it as we can't get past the pit, but we hope to find the thread again along another passage! Would you join us and help us look!" The beast fell silent for a while as if considering what he had been asked as the standoff continued. Finally, he spoke, "Are you children of Adikia?" Estella spoke up again, "We were stolen by Adikia to work in his mine, now he has set us free!" Again, the Minotaur fell quiet taking his time to process what had been said, before answering, "I am a friend to the stolen children of Adikia. I will help you. You look hungry, follow me!" The beast turned around and disappeared into the dark, and with some trepidation, Estella and Artemis followed. After travelling along a couple more passages, they found the tunnel opened up into a chamber which had luminous moss covering the floor, giving off a dim green glow and illuminating the passage. In the far corner, sat two more children who looked familiar. "Eric, Michael, is that you?" asked Artemis. "It is!" replied Eric. The four children hugged as both Eric and Michael explained the kindly Minotaur had saved them when they had become lost in the labyrinth. Both Artemis and Estella had thought the boys had perished in the pit and were very happy to see them alive and well. The Minotaur provided some mushrooms to eat whilst they rested, and they spoke more about the thread leading the way out of the labyrinth. It was decided the party would look in each passage for the thread, and they all set off to do so with great hopes. The many passages of the labyrinth are all interconnected in a complex and confusing manner. Designed to confuse, they walked around and around the maze, going in circles most of the time. Finally, after some hours, Eric caught sight of the thread running along the edge of one passage, "I've found it!" he announced with glee. "Good, now one end will lead to the pit with snakes and the other end will lead us all out of the labyrinth.", said Artemis with conviction. With that, the group followed the thread along the winding passages as it led them hopefully in the right direction. Estella was the first to notice the change to the walls of the passages, as they grew drier, "Look, touch the walls, they are drier! This means we are close to the surface.", she said with a smile. True enough, shortly later, the tunnel opened up into daylight, and the group stood on the verge, where daylight met shadow, allowing their eyes to slowly adjust to the brightness of day. The Minotaur felt a great fear of the light after spending so many years being trapped and living within the darkness of the labyrinth. "You are free to go to your homes now!" he said to the children. "And you are too!" said Estella. "I have no home; people fear me and will kill me as a monster. I must stay in the labyrinth!", "No, that's not right. We will tell the people that you saved and helped us!" begged the children. Eventually, after much begging, the Minotaur gingerly agreed to join the children as they walked to the village they could see in the distance, across the valley.

A large wall had been built around the village to stop the Adikia, and guards posted at the gate stopped them all. Despite being hostile and concerned about the Minotaur's intentions, after the children explained their ordeal and how the Minotaur had helped them escape the Labyrinth, the guards called the council of respected townspeople, and it was decided to permit the Minotaur safe harbour. The children returned to their families, and the men of the village formed an army with a new leader, the Minotaur, who now proudly carried the golden spear Artemis had given him. It had been decided that the monster Adikia must be killed and the children of the mine freed, and the army set off across the valley towards the labyrinth and towards battle.

Incommunicado Paradox

Michael was in his fifties and, following the sad loss of his wife five years ago, the last thing he wanted was to see his daughter sad. But lately, every time she visited, he could see her heart was struggling with life. There was always some new comment about how her boyfriend was more interested in his work than in her, and how it all made her feel rejected by him. Michael liked Mike, as he was a polite young man, and he held no doubt that he would remain true to his daughter, Stacey. Therefore, in the early days, Michael had stuck up for Mike to his daughter, as he had been very happy that Mike wasn't another loser like so many of Stacey's previous boyfriends. However, things had changed over the past few months, and Michael could see the genuine heartache that she was now going through. This was why he offered differing words of advice today when Stacey had once more confided her deepest worries to her dad. "The heart wants what the heart wants, sweetheart, there is no rhyme or reason to it! If you are not happy with Mike. If he can't provide you with the feeling of being loved that you crave, then maybe he isn't the one for you!" Michael regretted saying the words as soon as they had come out, but it was the honest truth and having witnessed his only daughter so low recently, perhaps it was what she needed to hear. Certainly, something needed to change in their relationship.

Later that night, Mike had blown off their plans yet again in favour of his work. She was sick of her boyfriend's lack of interest in her; every time she shared her deepest feelings with him, he seemingly ignored her and continued talking about the latest happenings in the field of theoretical physics! It was all too much for poor Stacey, who, armed with her father's words of wisdom and desperately feeling the need for the warmth and comfort of a caring relationship, decided to make a change. 'Twelve months on and we are barely anything more than friends!', she thought to herself whilst flicking through images of Mike on her smartphone. "I don't care if he is smart, I need more than this!" she said out loud and pulled up her texting app and started typing, "It's over between us! Don't speak to me again!" After typing in the message, her finger hovered over the send button as she reconsidered whether she really did want to end their relationship. After a further moment of thought, she felt the same old heartache again. No, she needed more than Mike could give her, she thought, and her finger hit the button, and in an instant the message was sent out across the mobile network towards Mike. Or at least that was what she thought!

The first signs that anything was wrong were when cosmonaut Ivan Venktill observed what he later described as "an unprecedented glitch due to unknown variables!" whilst observing the first operation of the new quantum entanglement chip aboard the latest Magna Tech Industries communication satellite! He saw what could only be described as a bubble of purply-blue photons engulf the chip before dissipating away into space in a brief shockwave. What actually occurred was something on a far greater scale than anyone could have possibly predicted. Well, at least any of the level-headed men of science. There were some who had predicted such a possible outcome of messing with nature on a quantum level. However, these Doctors of Science had suffered under the strain of performing such mental work in calculating quantum conundrums that they had started to develop some very peculiar habits, and all had classed them as crackpots.

The next morning, Stacey looked at her phone to see if Mike had messaged back, but when she looked, her message was nowhere to be seen. No log of sending a message even existed on her phone. Realising that she had been quite exhausted from crying last night, she wondered if perhaps she had just fallen asleep and maybe dreamt about sending the message. In any case, this morning she felt more positive about their relationship, and since the message was only part of a dream, she decided to send Mike a good morning text. "Good morning my love xxx", she typed and sent, before making herself a morning latte like she did every morning. Moments later, as her kettle clicked off, her phone buzzed and vibrated on the kitchen counter, signalling she had received a reply from Mike. Her mouth visibly opened in shock as she read his reply, "Who is this? You must have the wrong number!" Stacey was angry, confused and upset, and immediately messaged back, "This is Stacey, your girlfriend!" She wondered if she had sent that message last night after all and Mike was just behaving like this because he was pissed at her? Buzz buzz, went her phone, and she opened the screen to see a reply that hurt, "I don't have a girlfriend, please stop messaging!" Stacey knew right then that she had destroyed their relationship. Mike had clearly received the message last night and now was refusing to even acknowledge Stacey at all. After a few more messages where she explained her deep-seated worries and apologised for hurting him, Stacey found that Mike had blocked her number. Upset and alone, she pulled up her dad's number and rang, hoping to find a loving voice at the other end of the phone to calm her soul. To her surprise, a recorded voice announced, "We're sorry; you have reached a number that has been disconnected or is no longer in service!" Her heart fell out of her body and cracked open on the floor. Well, at least that is how it felt to Stacey, who was now also quite concerned about her father. Skipping work, she grabbed her car keys and headed out to her dad's house across the other side of town. Traffic was awful in the middle of rush hour, but eventually she reached calmer roads, and that is when she started to notice visible changes. Some roads had different surfaces, like concrete rather than the standard asphalt she had driven over yesterday! Not only that, but she was also sure some houses were painted differently. What was even worse, when she arrived at where her father's house had been, there was nothing! The house had vanished, as if it had never existed, and allotments filled the empty space where it had stood before. The inconceivable reconfiguration of her life all proved too much for Stacey, and she fainted.

Hours later, as she came to, a brightness stung her eyes. Slowly gaining focus, as you do when you come out of a deep sleep, she realised she was no longer in her car but in a hospital. Two men wearing black suits stood just inside. One was talking into his lapel, as if reporting to a commanding officer. Seconds later, another man in a black suit entered the room and approached Stacey. "Hello, I am Agent Smith from Magna Tech Industries, and I am here because you are suffering from temporal displacement!" It was clear that Stacey was just as confused as ever, so the agent continued, "Our logs show that you sent a message at twenty-three hundred hours last night to a person called Mike! Well, a very strange phenomenon that we are still trying to understand occurred after you sent this message! You see, your message happened to be the first message to use our new, faster-than-ever communications satellite. A satellite that makes use of quantum entanglement to send super-fast communications." Agent Smith paused for a moment as he wondered how he might possibly explain the delicacies of quantum mechanics to Stacey! "Unfortunately, some kind of glitch affected your message as the new chip settled into its role. This caused your message, it would appear, to not go to the Mike that you intended, but to your father, Michael instead!" Stacey's eyes opened as she tried to comprehend the agents' words, "But that makes no sense. What is really going on, how come Mike says he doesn't know me then, and where is my dad's house?" Agent Smith sighed and continued, "Well, we have the best minds working on this matter." As he spoke, he unintentionally rolled his eyes whilst thinking about the best minds that had been put to work on the project following the glitch; namely Dr Abaham, who worked best apparently whilst not wearing any trousers and Dr Henkl who insisted on wearing a foil hat to stop aliens from reading or controlling his mind. "Yes, we have the best minds working on this issue, and it turns out that your message was subjected to something which is unique to quantum mechanics! Now, in our reality, time is a constant. We exist in only one place in time, whilst in quantum mechanics, time can be looked at as existing in all places at once!" The puzzled look still plagued Stacey's face, so he continued in vain to explain what had actually occurred, "Your message didn't reach you father last night, it actually reached your father twenty-five years ago, when he was dating a girl called Stacey, a girl you are named after, your mother! Well, it would appear that upon receiving this message, your father broke up with your mother!" Stacey thought the agent was talking nonsense to her and she voiced as much, "That makes no sense, that can't be true!", "You are, of course, right, this simply doesn't make any sense, but nonetheless it appears to have happened, and this set of strange circumstances has caused a paradox! For if your message caused the breakup of your parents twenty-five years ago, then you haven't been born and couldn't have sent that message! But you are here, do exist and did send the message despite this!" The information was slowly sinking in, but she instinctively couldn't accept it. "So what? You are telling me I was born without a mother or a father! That my father's house never existed, despite the fact that I have been there a million times!" It was no surprise that Stacey was so very agitated, after all, no one in the history of mankind had ever been put through this kind of torture before. "I am truly your friend and want to help you as much as I can, but you have to accept this is a whole new ballgame and although I am very concerned for you this situation has posed a great threat to the very fabric of space time and quite frankly all we can do is watch and see what happens over the next twenty-four hours!" As Stacey realised a little of what had been said, she understood that she had never been born and her parents had simply never been. This caused a severe anxiety response and in a highly upset mood she lashed out at the agent, who due to his training was simply able to move out of her way as she lunged for him whilst at the same time moving in a position where he could restrain her allowing a doctor to administer a sedative which made her drift off to sleep.

She was tumbling through space, somehow breathing as she floated high above the Earth. A screen appeared ahead of her, and as she moved towards it, the stars around her blurred. She flew with greater and greater speed at the screen, eventually pressing hard up against it before then passing through it into a reflection of the universe. The screen lit up with images from her life, of birthday parties, holidays and even the sad funeral of her mother. It showed how she had met Mike, and then she sent the message. There was a flash of purply-blue, then the screen started rewinding. As time went backwards, parts of the universe disappeared from around her as she hung there in space, her eyes glued to the screen. Faster and faster the images went, further and further back in time as more and more of the universe disappeared from around her, leaving white holes in space. Until the screen reached the point when her father received the message, and then the screen went into a static white noise display, and Stacey found herself surrounded completely by white emptiness.

Six hours had passed at the hospital, and Stacey remained unresponsive, having passed into a coma of some kind after receiving the mild relaxant administered by the doctor. There was no physical reason for the coma, in fact, the relaxant should not have even put Stacey to sleep. In truth, Stacey was now a person out of time, and until the universe decided what it should do with this innocent victim of the paradox, it had felt keeping her in a coma was the more merciful option.

Agent Smith felt the urge for another nicotine hit, and with that went outside and lit up a cigarette. As he inhaled deeply, he felt the smoke relax his mind and give him the moment's calm he needed. He chatted with the other agents, who had been posted outside as security, when suddenly a brilliant light from above surrounded them as they stood. Looking up with their hands shielding their eyes, it was clear that something was approaching. Defenceless against what they were witnessing, the men stood motionless as a V-class Warrior ship landed right in front of them. Suddenly, steam, illuminated by the bright lights from within the ship, billowed out from either side. The ship rumbled, and a panel section opened on the bottom of the ship, and a long gangway slowly lowered to the ground. The steam had filled the air and all but entirely clouded the view of the gangway. After a moment, the steam cleared, and a figure walked forward, silhouetted by the light of the ship. The agents, who were secretly scared out of their wits, remembered their training and mentally prepared themselves for first contact. The figure walked to the end of the gangway and took a moment. He looked all around and then focused his attention on the agents standing a little way ahead of him, "I am called Geod the watcher! Your species has caused a tear through the fabric of spacetime, of which I am the guardian!" Lifting his laser gun from his side, he continued, "Prepare to feel my wrath!"

Quadrennial Contest

Pomposity and arrogance accompanied every event of the guild, but by far the most revered and pompous occasion was the quadrennial contest. This was a contest that occurred every four years and had a history dating back thousands of years.

You see, in vampiric culture, there are two sub-forms of vampire, much as in humanity, there exist different sub-types of people. In vampiric form, these exist as the go-getters and leaders who rise to the top along with all the wealth and estate that accompanies such. Then there are the others, the more subservient who stall in their accomplishments at much lesser levels. For those few vampires who had risen, life always seemed to become somewhat more predictable and quite unchallenging very quickly indeed. Their get-up-and-go attitude suddenly and metaphorically finds itself pressed hard up against a most elegantly crafted, beautiful glass wall, having achieved everything there was to achieve. In such an existential crisis, the elite had long ago created this contest as a means of entertaining their need for challenge. You see, the four highest vampires of the guild would select and sponsor an indifferent human, selling the poor sap on a fantastic notion. The sponsor would provide superb financial support to their candidate. The support would encounter anything needed to allow the human to rise to the very top of their field. Then, at the end of the four years, they would return to the location the candidate knew only as the guild of established businessmen to announce their achievements and be honoured by the guild. Humans knew nothing about vampires, as such creatures existed only in myth and fantasy. This lack of knowledge was not so much down to the ignorance of humankind, but was strictly ordered that such invisibility must remain under vampiric lore. Any action a vampire took that revealed themselves to the humans was punished harshly via incarceration without blood for one or more centuries, depending on the level of publicity caused. Therefore, vampires, naturally, kept themselves hidden, and their prey, humans, were, for the most part, ignorant about the peril they faced nightly.

This year, Ezri Datum, a beautiful young lady who showed much promise in the field of chemical engineering, had been chosen by the newest member of the guild, Goethe Bloom. Goethe had been the chief executive of a local authority, but after being turned, he had risen in vampiric society faster and bloodier than any other member of the guild. Within the very small timeframe of one hundred years, he had gained a place upon the guild's board, a feat which had previously been unheard of, as all others had existed as high-level vampires for a thousand years or more before being offered a place upon the board. However, as I said, Goethe's rise had been fast and bloody as his insatiable quest for power and bloodshed compelled him. To the extent of killing Alaine Drax, an existing board member, effectively creating an opening for himself that the other board members were simply too fearful of Goethe to deny him. Since such a historic rise, Goethe had plateaued as there simply was no higher for him to reach in vampiric society, and thus, he had focused upon the quadrennial contest as his main source of self-satisfaction. In the last one hundred years, Goethe's champions had won ninety-nine times. This year, he relished the notion of winning for the one hundredth time, which again would be another notch in his belt, gaining him the coveted centennial cup. Vampires, in general cared not a jot for the humans they lavished their finances upon, after all they were humans, stinking, obtuse humans, whose only value was like that of a pawn being used in a game, somewhat like a cat would play with a mouse, toying with it before snapping its neck.

Once the contest was complete and the winner announced, and after all of the pompous ceremony, the contestants would be invited back for a private ceremony, and that simply provided time for any members of the public to leave the guild and for the streets to empty. The private ceremony was purely a guise for what would become a night of toyful hunting for the guild. The sponsors would expose their true selves to the contestants during this private function and then permit them to run in fear through the night. The vampires follow, laughing and deliberately knock over bins and throw stones against metal gates, etc, to simply disturb their prey more. Taking great enjoyment from what was more of a spectator sport than a true hunt, eventually, the vampires would close in and kill each contestant with varying levels of speed and torture. Every contestant, that is, except the contest winner, who would be offered a choice of an instant painless death or of immortality with them taking their earned place as a vampire under their sponsor's tree. This is how Goethe had been turned into a vampire all those years earlier.

Tonight was the winner's celebration, and despite being aimed mostly at the accomplishments of the current contestants, next year's entrants were also called forward. Joining each of the four sponsors on the stage, they swore an oath to the rules in honour of the contest. So it was that Ezri found herself announcing her allegiance. She had come to the attention of Goethe only quite recently, having already won a host of business awards in chemical engineering, without the vast financial support that came with a rich sponsor. Her achievements included developing a plethora of successful drugs for treating the wide variety of diseases plaguing humanity. Ezri was already set well on her way to becoming a leader within her field. Goethe, of course, envisioned the precious and revered centennial cup, which was gifted to only the very few who had successfully won one hundred games in a row. With this foremost in his mind and without questioning anything about her past, he offered to be her sponsor for this most secret of business contests. Her fellow entrants all showed great interest and excitement to receive such financial support and gain over the next four years, and all accepted the rules and proceeded to get drunk with visions of great riches and academic successes riding high on their minds. Not wishing to seem out of place, Ezri aped this behaviour and joined in with the celebrations. For them all, tomorrow was the start of a new life, a life of entitlement which would allow them to fulfil their dreams and blaze like bright stars within their respective endeavours.

For Ezri, winning in the field of chemical engineering came easily and quite honestly, she would have become a true leader in this field without any financial support. But she had accepted the support, and in the years that came, she made good use of it in funding vital research. In the final year of the contest, as her work over the past four years culminated, she requested larger and larger financial inputs from Goethe. She had focused on successfully developing a safe, non-invasive alternative to chemotherapy. After which accomplishment, she was honoured as the chemist who cured cancer. Not only did she save many billions of lives, but in great respect of this astonishing accomplishment, she was further awarded the Nobel Prize for chemistry and with that, basically clinched the winner's title of the contest. Just as she had always intended to do.

That year's ceremony shortly came around, and Ezri was heralded as the winner, with all the usual splendour and pomp. She smiled and showed how excited and thankful she was for the support she had received and even attributed her achievement to that of her sponsor's support. Everything seemed to be just fine. Then, after the public left, she found herself at the closed private after-party, held for contestants and sponsors only. Initially, little seemed different, but then, for Ezri and for each of the contestants, their lives of splendour suddenly churned and changed into their worst nightmare as the guild revealed their true vampiric nature and the quadrennial hunt began. Frightened out of their minds along with incredible feelings of doom, the small group of four fled out of the guild building and poured onto the empty streets of downtown London. The empty streets formed perfect locations for the vampires to play with their night's entertainment. Every now and then, the group would start to calm and develop a feeling of safety, as they felt they had successfully escaped their pursuers. It was at those moments, especially, that a vampire would appear briefly and nudge or lightly claw one of them, re-instilling the fear ever greater in the hearts of the scared prey. So, it went on, hour after hour. The group, by the end of it, had all but lost their minds from the intense trauma and overdoses of adrenaline being pumped around their frail mortal bodies. Then, as the night drew to a close, ahead of the dawning sunlight, the cat and mouse game came to an end as each sponsor caught and took down their prey, concluding the contest and their night's entertainment. Only one last act was required, and so, Goethe, with one long, bony, claw-like hand tight around Ezri's neck, he spoke the words used again and again over and over across a millennium, "As winner, you have a choice! Instant death or join us in immortality!" As he spoke, he traced Ezri's jugular vein using a single long pointed fingernail from his other hand, as if anticipating the process of draining her body of blood. Usually, a desperate panic would come over any human faced with this dilemma, and most would opt for death or simply pass out and be killed anyway. Ezri, however, was different in this respect and calmly answered to Goethe's surprise, "I choose immortality!" Of course, ceremonial rules laid down within the guild's very fabric specified that the sponsor must accept such a request, and despite some confusion within Goethe's mind, he tilted Ezri's neck and sank his sharp teeth deep into her jugular. In drinking a little of her blood as he passed on his cursed nature, he found something was very different with Ezri. Her blood wasn't at the normal body temperature! Instead, it was cold, damn cold. Goethe pulled back, but it was too late! He realised Ezri was already a vampire, and what was worse, one who had treated her vampiric nature through her intuitive knowledge of chemistry. A smile flickered wickedly across Ezri's face, "Now do you remember me?" Her words haunted Goethe as he felt his strength weaken in his body. "I am Ezri, Kitsune of the east and one hundred years ago, you turned me into a vampire! I was pregnant then and my child was stillborn, neither dead nor alive, but with an immortal sleeping sickness upon her! This is my revenge!" She plunged a tainted knife deep into Goethe's chest and through his heart. "Now, you will die! Having never fed on human blood, I will be released from your course!" Goethe fell to the floor from the fatal stab, and Ezri and the remaining members of the guild watched as slowly the immortality left his body, and he turned to nothing more than ash. Ezri was instantly freed of the curse, and to her, what was more important, was that her daughter Emi would now also be free and alive. "What makes you think you can survive this attack upon the guild?" demanded Aran, the tallest of the vampires. "Is it not in your rules that you must allow me to go free, having bested my sponsor? Your rules are all you have, so you must abide by them!" Ezri responded and promptly metamorphosed into a fox and ran away down the street into the remaining shadows of the night. The vampires looked upon each other in contemplation of what had just occurred, "She is right, of course, rules are rules!", one said. "He was from very bad stock anyway!" another offered as they all felt a certain levity that Goethe, whom they had all feared, had unfortunately suffered a fate of his own bringing. "That concludes this year's game! As Goethe is no longer with us, he forfeits the contest, and I remain holder of the centennial cup! Now let us get out of these damp streets and return to the guild and hold a toast to remember poor Goethe!" With that, the vampires wisely chose to conclude this matter and left for the guild.

Bibliography

Solnit, R. (2014)'The solitary stroller in the city'. Source: Solnit, R. (2014)'The solitary stroller in the city', *in Wanderlust: A History of Walking*. London: Granta Publications, pp. 175-195.

Artemis, D & Varakis, A (2006) *Antigone*. London: Methuen Publishing Ltd.

Bruce, J & Clapton, E. (1967) *Sunshine of your love*. New York City: Reaction/Polydor (UK), Atco (US)